SLAYING SEASON

James Laabs

First American Publishing

First American Publishing
1102 Wedgewood Drive
Waukesha, WI 53186
Email jameslaabs@yahoo.com

This novel is a work of fiction. The characters, names, incidents, dialogue and plot are the products of the author's imagination or are used fictitiously. Any resemblance to actual persons or events is purely coincidental.

Certain real-life businesses and universities may be named in this book as a means of plot development or to portray a more realistic backdrop for the story. All events, incidents and activities involving those businesses and universities are completely fictitious.

ISBN 978-0-9767599-3-5

ACKNOWLEDGEMENT

I want to express both my gratitude and unending love to my fiancé Tracy. Her encouragement kept me going over the months that it took to write this book, and her honest feedback kept me aiming for the stars in my writing .

I couldn't have done it without you, baby.

Major Characters

Jake Goodman – Sports Information Director
Harvey Elwood – Athletic Director
Molly Bennett – Assistant Athletic Director, Women's Sports
Milt Atkins – Assistant Athletic Director, Men's Sports
Jennifer Stewart – Graduate Assistant to the Athletic Director
Ellen Benjamin – Girlfriend of Jake Goodman
John Rose – Head sports reporter for the *State Journal-Register*
Sheila Elwood – Socialite wife of Harvey Elwood
Donald "Slim" Haskins – Head football coach at Lincoln State
Steve Jefferies – Head basketball coach at Lincoln State
Eduardo "Eddie" Martin – Detective, Springfield PD
Ken McGrew – Ex-cop and current private investigator

Lincoln State University Football Schedule
(H- Home, A-Away)

Mid-Central University (H)
Michigan State University (A)
UCLA (A)
University of Tennessee (A)
Eastern Carolina (H)
Akron University (A)
University of Cincinnati (A)
University of Texas-El Paso (A)
New Mexico State University (A)
University of Tulsa (H)
University of Florida (A)
Iowa State University (H)

Chapter One

The Athletic Director looked at the resume for the fiftieth time and, try as he might, could find nothing to dislike about Jacob "Jake" Goodman. He had the brains, a commendable service record in the Marines, good looks and came from a solid family. If only there was a giant red flag that popped out – then he'd have a reason to not hire the kid. That would make life a lot easier, since he would have loved to use the Sports Information Director job opening to pay back one of the many favors that needed paying back.

As it was, Jake Goodman was the only son of one of the top financial backers of Lincoln State University. And when it came to doing favors for large donors to university athletics, money didn't just talk – it shouted.

Turning back to Jake Goodman's resume, he ticked off the points. Goodman had a degree in journalism from good old Lincoln State, so he was an alumnus. Not a necessity but a strong point in his favor. Jake was white, and although the Athletic Director would deny it with his last breath, there was no way he was hiring anyone of color into a responsible position in the athletic department. In the little corner of the university that Harvey Elwood ruled, the color of authority was lily white and that's how Harvey planned to keep it.

Harvey sighed loudly as he pictured what would happen if he backed another candidate. Jake's father would go crying straight to the Board of Trustees and Harvey would make a fool out himself trying to defend any other choice. Jake Goodman had an immaculate background and was qualified enough that his father's clout pushed him to the top of the heap for the Sports Information Director position.

The Athletic Director had even gone so far as to hire (with cash so there wouldn't be a trail) a private eye who he sometimes used for discrete dirt-digging. The P.I. came up empty. In fact, the investigative report was so boring that it almost put him to sleep. This kid was a straight arrow – not so much as a speeding ticket. Since Jake had returned from his tour of duty in Iraq three months earlier, he behaved like a priest. He drank an occasional beer now and then, but when he found himself at a party where weed and coke came out he politely declined and found a reason to leave early.

There was no question about it, no other candidate matched up nearly as well as Jake Goodman. Harvey was stuck, and he would be unable to pay back any favors with this hire.

Harvey was about to let out another sigh when there was a knock on his door. "Come in!" he shouted. It was Molly Bennett, the dyke who managed the women's side of the athletic department. The athletic department was split in two, with two Assistant Directors. One was responsible for men's sports and one for women's sports, and both reported to Harvey. Although he and Molly didn't see eye-to-eye on a lot of things, he respected her because she was a very competent administrator, a quality that was sorely needed on the women's sports side of the department. It took a hard-nose like Molly to stretch miniscule budgets and build support for sports that didn't draw flies when it came to paid attendance.

"So, how is it going with the Sports Information Director position?" Molly asked, "Have you made a decision?"

Harvey slid Jake's resume across his spacious mahogany desk toward her. "Here's our man – Jake Goodman. He's the offspring of Stan Goodman, one of Lincoln State's biggest contributors."

Molly scanned the resume quickly while she mumbled. "Hmmm...degree from Lincoln State, good...war hero, huh? That'll sit well with our older alum...I see he did a couple of internships with the *Peoria Journal-Star* and the WICS-TV sports department here in Springfield. That will help. Not as much experience as I'd like to see, but he looks like a decent choice, Harvey. Let's get him on the payroll so we can start getting some stuff in the paper about women's soccer. The season starts in a few weeks and it's one of my only sports that actually sells a few tickets."

"I'm bringing him in to talk about a job offer tomorrow. But I wanted to make sure you're on board with this."

"He looks great to me, what did Milt have to say about him?" Molly asked. Milt Atkins was – at least in title – her equal, responsible for overseeing the day-to-day operations of the men's side of the department. In reality, Harvey kept Milt under his thumb and made most of the decisions, relegating Milt to being a well-paid paper pusher.

"Milt isn't a part of this decision, Molly, so if he doesn't like it he can go fuck himself."

Molly gave a tiny evil smile. It was time to tease old Harvey a little, which she enjoyed doing, "Or he may go running to the Board of Trustees to squeal on you, he certainly isn't afraid to do that."

Harvey frowned, "The next time he goes over my head, it will be his last official act as an Assistant Director. I'll demote him so far down he'll be reporting to the little girls who peddle popcorn at your soccer games."

Molly laughed, "You know what, Harvey? I believe you'd do it. Milt has been a thorn in your side from the first day you met him. And you wouldn't have an argument from me. In fact, I could use the change of scenery and handle men's sports instead of pinching pennies with the girls."

"And you would be damn good at it too, Molly. I'll keep you in mind if and when I can shake Milt loose from the department. In the meantime, go count some soccer balls or something and let me get back to work."

Molly took Harvey's good natured dismissal with a smile. "OK, Harv. Bring the kid over to meet me when he's ready to get to work."

"The annual kickoff picnic is next Saturday," Harvey said, "I figured that would be a good place to have him meet everyone."

The kickoff picnic was usually held on the Saturday before registration began for the fall semester, before the non-athlete student body descended on the campus. It was a chance for athletes in all sports to cut loose a bit and get themselves in a frame of mind to attend class, study and play at top level in their chosen sport (although not necessarily in that order).

Harvey picked up the phone and dialed Jake Goodman's cell phone. "Jake! Harvey Elwood here. I'd like you to come over tomorrow morning. I want to make you the new Sports Information Director for Lincoln State."

Jake put down the phone, smiled with satisfaction and gave a subdued fist pump. The Lincoln State job was a perfect place to start his career. The only reservation he had about taking the job was that his dad had thrown his influence into the hiring process. Jake worried that he would be viewed as some trust-fund punk who relied on his family's wealth and clout to get ahead. People who knew him at all recognized that Jake was determined to make his own way in the world – if the people at Lincoln State thought he was a rich kid slacker who was going to coast on his dad's wealth, they were badly mistaken. That's why he had joined the Marines right after graduation. He wanted to get out from under his dad's massive shadow and the best way to do that was to put his career off for a few years and join the service.

The day he enlisted was still clear in Jake's mind. He had graduated from Lincoln State just the month before and found that job prospects were pretty slim for new grads. Although Jake got top grades, journalism majors outnumbered job openings by about 5-to-1 and a degree from a small school in Springfield, Illinois held zero prestige with the big media outlets in Chicago or St. Louis. After he struck out in the job market, the last thing Jake wanted was to sit around Springfield doing nothing, and since his dad forbade him to take any job that was "beneath him," joining the Marines seemed like the easy way out.

He remembered that it was a sunny, warm summer day when he walked in the door of the family's spacious house and announced he was leaving for boot camp within the week. His mother made a strange gurgling sound, turned ashen white and fainted; Jake still shuddered when he recalled the clunk her head made when she hit the floor. His father paused from screaming at him for a few seconds when she fell, took a quick glance to make sure his wife was conscious (she was) and then resumed his tirade. Of course, Stan Goodman offered to "pull some strings" and persuade someone to misplace Jake's enlistment papers. Jake's refusal of that offer was received with bulging neck veins and even louder shouting by his father.

It turned out that the Marines was as positive an experience as fighting in a war could be. Jake returned home with a small box full of medals and felt like he had taken a huge step toward proving his own worth, independent of his family. He also had the good fortune of picking up some excellent experience working for the Marine's public information office for five months. Jake injured his leg in battle and a commanding officer, who had taken a liking to him, assigned him to journalism duty until he was ready to return to his unit. Taglines on quite a few stories read "by Jake Goodman," and those would hopefully prove invaluable in landing a journalism job. Jake was brimming with confidence and optimism when he was discharged.

Now he landed the Sports Information Director position for a Division I athletic program; a job that anyone would grab in a second as the starting point for a journalism career. Obviously his father had put in a good word for him, but Jake could live with that.

Jake pulled into a parking spot marked "reserved for athletic department staff only," slammed the door of his hybrid sports car, checked his tie in the side mirror, and walked into the athletic offices. The colors of the Abes (the Lincoln State nickname, for Abraham Lincoln who was born in the area) were royal blue and gray, so the reception area was covered in rich blue carpet with gray highlights. To his left, Jake noticed a floor-to-ceiling glass case with several sports trophies won by the Abes over the years.

"Jake Goodman, to see Harvey Elwood," his said, flashing his brightest smile at the receptionist. It's never too early to start winning people over, he thought. The cute, thirty-ish receptionist gave her best smile back and said, "Go right in

Jake, he's expecting you."

Harvey Elwood's office was spacious and recently redecorated. As Jake shook hands with Harvey and sat down, he couldn't help but be impressed with the view from the huge window. The athletic department offices were in a building located just off one of the corners of the football stadium. The building was built with a small footprint but was four stories tall. Harvey's corner office on the top floor overlooked the stadium and football field. Of course, blue and gray dominated the décor'; Jake played a mental game to count the items in the office that weren't blue or gray and was able to tally them on one hand with fingers to spare. Harvey himself wore a gray suit with a royal blue tie. It brought to mind the joke that Jake's dad told him about Harvey being so loyal to Lincoln State that if he cut himself he'd bleed royal blue instead of red.

The meeting went smoothly. The money was all right and Jake was excited for the chance to go to work for his alma mater. His first introduction to the world of Lincoln State athletic administration would be at the annual kickoff picnic the next day.

Chapter Two

"Are you sorry you got yourself into this yet?" boomed the voice of Donald "Slim" Haskins, head coach of the Lincoln State Abes football team. Jake smiled and paused before answering. Whoever hung the nickname "Slim" on Donald Haskins must have been either blind or had a cruel sense of humor, Jake thought. Haskins was about six feet tall but had 300 pounds packed onto his wide frame.

"Actually I'm looking forward to getting to work," Jake answered politely, "and one of the first things on my list is to work on getting some press for your team. The season starts three weeks from today if I'm not mistaken."

"You got that right, boy. And we need some publicity – season ticket sales dropped off a bit this year so it's up to you to get some asses in those seats."

"That's what I'm here to do, so I'll plan on getting together in your office with you Monday afternoon right after practice ends," Jake said decisively in hopes of ending the conversation as quickly as possible.

"Okeydokey. See you then, junior."

Just then, a familiar face ambled up to him and Haskins. Jake recognized him as Steve Jefferies, the men's basketball coach for the Abes. Steve Jefferies was polar opposite of Slim Haskins. He was tall, good looking and in great shape. He also had a personality that was both easy going but serious at the same time. He was well-spoken and intelligent with just the right touch of genuine enthusiasm about the university and his basketball team.

The results of the football team and basketball team also were exact opposites: Slim Haskins' football team was coming off a 1-and-10 season with their only win coming against perennial doormat Northeast Missouri. On the other hand, the Abes basketball team made the "Big Dance" three years running and routinely sold out every game while the football team struggled to build a following.

The coaches were both stereotypes in their own way. Slim Haskins was an "old school" coach, one of the last of a dying breed. He was abrasive, didn't get along well with the media, and wasn't well liked by alumni, fans or his own players. Haskins was typical of coaches being replaced by a new generation of coaches like Steve Jefferies. Jake recalled reading an interview with Gene Corrigan, the former commissioner of the Atlantic Coast Conference. Corrigan said, "Most schools have come to grips with the fact that there aren't many Bear Bryant's out there anymore. Universities are hiring coaches not just based on their success at diagramming X's and O's on a locker room blackboard, but also on their ability to appease alumni, graduate players and represent their universities with distinction. The guys who succeed in the coaching business are intelligent and well spoken."

The new breed of coaches studied psychology and public relations to better handle their players, the media, fans and the wide range of other people they came in contact with as a major college coach. Slim Haskins was a dinosaur and everyone, from the Board of Trustees to Slim himself, knew it. This was the last year of his contract, and Slim Haskins realized that it would take a great year to keep his job after this season.

Jake couldn't help but notice that the tension between Haskins and Steve Jefferies was extremely high.

"So Steve-O," Slim said, "I saw your star forward driving a new SUV last week. I wonder how he got himself such a nice car."

"He saved the money from his summer job for a down payment," Steve Jefferies answered calmly, "the first thing I did when I saw him with it was ask him how he got it. Then I made some calls to verify his story and it checked out. That's how we do things in my program – on my team players know they're accountable. You ought to try it sometime."

Haskins' round face flushed bright red, "Well, yeah, it's easy for you to keep tabs on fifteen players; I have over ninety players on the football team that I have to keep in line."

"You also have eight assistant coaches to help you."

Jake didn't want to be caught in the middle of a discussion that was growing more heated by the moment, so he interrupted. "Coach Jefferies, I've already set up a meeting to go over the publicity plan for football this year," he said, "as soon as I get the fall sports going and the dust settles we should get together about basketball."

"That works for me," Steve Jefferies said, just as eager to avoid a shouting match with Slim Haskins in front of the entire athletic department, "give me a call in a few weeks."

Slim Haskins used the opportunity to stomp off in the direction of the beer keg, and Steve Jefferies ambled off in another direction. Molly Bennett took the opportunity to introduce herself to Jake.

"Just the man I need to get to know," Molly said with a smile as she thrust out her hand. "I'm Molly Bennett, women's assistant A.D. We have a lot of work to do in a very short amount of time."

"I couldn't agree more," Jake said. As they chatted, Jake recalled his father's assessment of the key people in the athletic department. Dad seemed to have missed the mark on Molly Bennett, who he described to Jake as "a humorless broad with a giant chip on her shoulder." On the contrary, Jake's first impression was that Molly was funny, competent and very smart. They agreed to meet first thing Monday morning in her office.

As he talked with Molly, Jake noticed Harvey Elwood walking away from the picnic area, heading down the trail that led to the crew team's boathouse. The Lincoln State campus was adjacent to a small lake which the crew teams used for rowing practice, and the boathouse was nestled in the trees by the shore. The University was surprisingly a national power in the sport of crew, thanks to a world-class facility funded by a graduate who rowed for Lincoln State while in college and hit it big in the 1990s in computer software.

A slight, skinny man in his late forties approached Jake and Molly. He was wearing gray shorts with a royal blue Lincoln State t-shirt and had a broad smile on his face. "Jake, I'm Milt Atkins, the Assistant Athletic Director. Glad to have you with us."

"One of two Assistant Athletic Directors," Molly said, "the other one would be me."

Milt Atkins laughed good-naturedly, "How could I ever forget, Molly? You remind me every day. Jake, we are looking forward to seeing what you can do, especially for the football program. Hopefully you'll do better than your predecessor."

Molly and Jake both grimaced. Everyone in the athletic department knew the story of the previous Sports Information Director at Lincoln State and how his career ended.

Football attendance the previous year was dismal with the stands half-full for many games. Students, normally the most loyal attendees, were not even showing up. They had discovered it was more fun to drink at their frat house or local bar than to sneak booze into the stadium and be subjected to another woeful performance by the Abes.

With pressure mounting to boost attendance, the desperate Sports Information Director came up with a creative idea to promote the next home game: he convinced the Springfield Zoo to co-sponsor a "Day at the Zoo" event at the football game. How could it go wrong? The zoo would get some publicity and dads could drag their kids to the game and kill two birds with one stone; watch a football game and let the kids see some zoo animals.

As the players left the field at halftime, the zookeepers paraded their animals onto the artificial turf. It was a grand and amazing sight as an elephant, tiger, zebra, horses and a dozen other animals pranced around the playing field.

Unfortunately, no one anticipated the obvious result of having several nervous large animals in a confined area. As the beasts were led off the playing surface, they left behind enormous piles of poop. Giant turd mounds littered the field like smelly land mines.

Since getting the zoo animals on and off the field had used up all of the time allotted for the halftime break, the referees and media producers were calling for the game to start the moment the last animal stepped out of the stadium. In the meantime, athletic department interns were dispatched to find buckets, water, hoses, anything that could possibly be used to clean the field. Their frantic efforts resulted in perhaps one-tenth of the meadow muffins being removed, but many piles remained as the teams lined up for the second half kick-off.

Very few people remember the score, or even who won the game. But the second half would go down in history as one of the low points of the athletic program at Lincoln State University. Players were streaked with zoo animal *ordure* and fans in the lower rows of seats gagged on the smell. Coaches were holding towels doused with analgesic rub over their faces to try to mask the horrendous odor. The newspaper reported sightings of small children in the stands vomiting the soda and popcorn they had consumed during the first half. The most memorable play involved a player from the opposing team stretching to catch a pass, making the catch and then sliding on his belly for fifteen yards through a wet turd pile, leaving a long, brown streak on the field.

The Sports Information Director was excused from his position the very next day by unanimous vote at a special Sunday morning meeting of the Athletic Board. Harvey was chastised by the Board but shifted the vast majority of the blame with some smooth talking and finger pointing. He was so shell-shocked that he assigned Sports Information duties to various administrators and put off hiring a new S.I.D. and promotions manager until the following summer.

***

Harvey took a quick look over his shoulder as he approached the boathouse. No one had followed him down the trail from the picnic area. He pulled his keys from his pocket, quickly unlocked the door and stepped inside. Suddenly two arms and two legs wrapped around him from behind and he felt a wet, warm tongue in his ear.

"Did'ja miss me?" asked Jennifer Stewart.

"Can't you tell?" he replied as he removed her from his back, spun her around and thrust his hips into her.

"Oooh, yes...I can tell!"

Harvey gently pushed Jennifer into the large pile of nylon boat covers that were in the corner of the large room. Sleek wooden boats that were little more than empty hulls and a hundred oars of various lengths were stored all around the room on steel racks. The outside walls had a few windows but Harvey and Jennifer felt secure knowing that no one had any reason to be anywhere near the boathouse on this day.

This was the first time they had seen one another in over two months and there was little foreplay. Jennifer moaned with pleasure as Harvey entered her and within a few minutes both of them had climaxed explosively. Now they lay in the pile of nylon fabric, entwined and both still breathing hard.

"Welcome back to the new school year, and congratulations on your promotion to Graduate Assistant to the Athletic Director," Harvey said.

Harvey had met Jennifer two years before, when she was a junior captain of the women's volleyball team. He was immediately struck by her unique good looks and maturity. Jennifer was everything that a fifty-year-old man needed. She was personable, fun, mature for her age and a sexual dynamo, at least compared to Harvey's near-frigid wife. Best of all, Jennifer understood discretion – a key attribute in a mistress if one was a married, high profile public figure.

When they started their affair, Jennifer accepted immediately that this was a fling with no long-term chance of leading somewhere. She was in her second year of grad school and would almost certainly leave in spring to start a career hundreds of miles away. She lived in the moment with no expectations about the future of their relationship, and that was one of the things that made her so attractive to Harvey.

As they lay on the soft nylon, sexually spent and totally relaxed, both heard a sound came from one of the windows, almost as if someone had tapped on the window. Harvey jumped up, pulled on his underwear and hurried to the window. There was no one outside. "Probably just a pine cone or a branch hit the window," he said to Jennifer. Yet, throughout the rest of the day he couldn't get rid of the feeling that someone had been watching them.

Chapter Three

Jake arrived precisely at 8 a.m. Monday to begin his first day on the job. The other athletic department staff members were still drifting in, but Harvey was waiting for Jake in the lobby to greet him with a broad smile and handshake.

"Welcome aboard, Jake! Let me give you the big tour of the place and then we'll get you settled in your office," Harvey said.

The athletic offices were modern, plush and professionally decorated. Blue and gray were the colors of choice, and memorabilia from various sports were scattered throughout the offices. Lincoln State had a streamlined athletic department staff compared to larger universities, with about twenty full-time administration and clerical staff, plus several part-time medical trainers from the university hospital and medical school faculty.

Most of the low-level work was done by interns who worked for little or no pay in exchange for course credit or an impressive line on their resumes. There were also a handful of graduate assistants, mostly ex-athletes working on graduate degrees or finishing their undergrad degrees, who were compensated with tuition grants or sometimes paid a small salary.

"How many sports does the university have?" Jake asked as they walked.

"Twenty-six total," Harvey said, "thirteen each for men and women. At Lincoln State, two sports – football and wrestling – are just for men, and two sports – volleyball and field hockey – are only open to women. We used to have fifteen men's sports and ten women's sports but Title IX took care of that."

Athletic equality was mandated in 1972 by a Federal law referred to as Title IX. While most discussion about the law is regarding college athletics, Title IX encompasses all educational opportunities and activities, from elementary school through higher education. Any institution that takes Federal money is bound by Title IX. But the law had the greatest impact on college sports. There was a major upheaval following passage of the law where many universities were forced to cut a number of men's sports in order to equalize the opportunities between men and women.

"Title IX and the NCAA have made it a royal pain in the ass to run an athletic program," Harvey sneered, "did you know, we have two full-time people in our Compliance Section who do nothing other than make sure we're following the rules. With that crook Slim Haskins running the football team, it sometimes seems like we need a third person just to keep tabs on the shit he tries to pull."

"But football is the main money-maker, isn't that right?"

"Yeah, football and men's basketball pretty much fund all the other sports, a few other sports like soccer and women's volleyball break even and in a good year maybe contribute a few bucks. But by and large we depend on football and basketball to keep us afloat. Well, here's your office. I'll send my assistant Jennifer in to make sure you get all the supplies you need, and she should be able to answer any other questions you have."

Jake stepped in, sat at his new desk and surveyed his small but comfortable work area. It was sparsely decorated and every work surface was empty. But Jake had a feeling that wouldn't last long. He picked up his phone, looked at the staff directory and dialed Molly's extension.

"Molly, Jake Goodman here. Are you ready to get together?"

"Give me about fifteen minutes and then come on over."

Jake looked up to see a perky, attractive girl standing in the office doorway. Jennifer Stewart introduced herself to Jake with a smile. "I'm a graduate assistant this academic year, working directly for Harvey. I remember you from your playing days on the basketball team. When I was in seventh grade my dad brought me to see some games that you played in. One of my friends had a crush on you."

"Wow, you make it sound like I'm ready for a wheelchair," Jake laughed.

Jennifer blushed and said, "No, I didn't mean it that way. But you have been away from Lincoln State for a few years and I just finished my playing career a year ago. So if you have any questions about what's been happening in the athletic pro-gram since you've been gone, let me know."

"Will do, and thanks. It was nice to meet you."

"Me too. I think you'll really like working here. Harvey is a great boss and a wonderful guy," Jennifer said as she left his office.

Molly was at her desk when Jake knocked and walked in. Her office was a small step down from Harvey's luxurious space, but was still pretty nice. Located on the fourth floor across the hall from Harvey's office, she too had a spacious window, but it faced away from the football field and instead had a panoramic view of the campus. Another difference was that Harvey had Jennifer Stewart plus another secretary who worked in a reception area outside of his office, while Molly's office door opened directly into the corridor. Molly and Milt shared a full-time clerical person and had one part-time graduate assistant assigned to them. Their assistants worked in a cubicle farm on the second floor.

As they were discussing the women's program, Jake asked

Molly how many athletic scholarships the women's program was allotted to grant.

"That depends on two things," Molly answered, "As you know, the NCAA is the governing national body for college sports. They set the maximum number of scholarships for each year for each sport. For instance, women's soccer has fourteen scholarships at most we can give out per year. Men's football can grant eighty-five scholarships. Of course, the football team has nearly a hundred players and the women's soccer team has less than twenty-five. The other factor is how many scholarships Lincoln State actually decides to grant; we don't have to give out the maximum each year. Take field hockey...believe it or not the NCAA limit is twelve, which seems like a lot for a minor sport. Harvey decided to only allow eight scholarships. Even though the tuition portion of a scholarship only costs the university an extra seat in a classroom, the cost of room and board can get out of hand, plus the tutoring and other services we provide to athletes."

"Is Harvey a good guy to work for? To be honest with you, he doesn't have much of a reputation with the alumni as a great business mind."

Molly pondered the question. Every Lincoln State fan knew the saga of Harvey Elwood. Harvey graduated from Lincoln State in the late 1960s, one of few athletes who excelled at multiple sports that he participated in. He received varsity letters in football, basketball and track – a feat that no one at Lincoln State had matched since, and in the age of sports specialization it was doubtful anyone ever would.

Coming out of Lincoln State, Harvey was a hot commodity and headed for the NFL and a pro football career – but instead of being picked in the NFL draft, he was drafted by Uncle Sam. After Vietnam he came home and played eight seasons in the NFL. After his football career ended, he drifted around to various jobs where he could capitalize on his name recognition.

Finally, in spring of 2000, the Athletic Director job opened up at Lincoln State. The Board of Trustees overlooked Harvey's shortcomings in administration skills and experience in favor of his well-known face, charismatic personality and fund raising ability. It turned out to be a good choice, especially during the first five or six years. The past few years, the poor performance of the football program was causing a growing wave of discontent and there were not nearly as many Lincoln State backers blinded by Harvey's fame and smile as when he started as Athletic Director.

Molly finally answered, "There are lots of things that make a person good in the Athletic Director job for a Division I university. Even Harvey would agree that his strong suit isn't shuffling papers. But he knows how to get along with all the people he has to get along with. Look at all the people he has to keep happy: the coaches, Board of Trustees, the media, his staff and of course the alumni, especially the important ones that make big donations. He hasn't done badly but that damned football team is dragging him down. Football is the key to success for any athletic program; it's the big money-maker. Those empty stands at football games are destroying Harvey's chances of keeping his job."

In less than two hours, Jake and Molly laid out the basics of a promotion and public relations plan for all of the fall women's sports. Jake was impressed with Molly's professional demeanor and efficiency. He left the meeting wondering if Molly wasn't the brains of the athletic program and Harvey was just the grinning, good-natured figurehead.

On Jake's afternoon schedule was the unpleasant task of meeting with Slim Haskins to lay out the public relations plan for the football season. The first game was less than three weeks away, so it was the highest priority. Most of the big projects, like the football media guidebook, were already completed and distributed to all sports reporters in Illinois. But without a hard push by Lincoln State to provide positive publicity for the football program, the local newspapers, radio and TV had already filled the information gap with some negative stories about the upcoming football season. Fan enthusiasm certainly was not at an all-time high, Jake thought ruefully.

The football offices and locker rooms were located in the stadium itself, which was connected by a breezeway to the athletic department building. The football stadium was typical of many college facilities; it was originally built in the mid-1900s but renovated and modernized many times over the years. In spite of that, the entrance to the football offices involved walking through the poorly lit, cavernous, concrete underbelly of the stadium.

"Well, well, if it isn't our newly minted sports information hotshot," Slim said in a taunting voice as he shook Jake's hand, "Come here to work some miracles for us?"

"That's what I'm here for, but it would really help the cause to have a good product on the field."

Befitting a head football coach, Slim changed from offense to defense instantly. "Hey, lighten up! The first kick-off hasn't even happened yet. It's too early to bury us. We've got a ton of seniors coming back. I think we have a shot to win the conference."

"One thing we need to address head-on is the rumor that you might not make it through the season if the Abes don't get off to a good start. I need to have some quotes from you to give to the press."

"Let me tell you something, kid. I'm not worried in the least about losing my job. I'm feeling pretty darn secure here. Old Slim Haskins has got himself an ace-in-the-hole. I'll bet you anything I'll still be sitting in this office next season, maybe even with a long-term contract."

Haskins' confidence seemed so out of place to Jake that he couldn't even respond. Was the coach delusional to think he had any sort of job security? Jake decided to move onto other items on his list of public relations tasks. He gave up on small talk and outlined his promotional plan in order to get Slim's approval on each point, hiding his eagerness to get out of the football coach's office as quickly as possible. Even with his effort to get the meeting done quickly, it was after 5:30 p.m. when Jake walked out of Slim's office, and the rest of the football offices and athletic department had the dimly lit emptiness of an office at night.

Getting out of the elevator on his floor, Jake nearly collided with Jennifer Stewart. His feelings were a bit hurt when she barely acknowledged him with a terse nod, and she hurriedly pressed the ground floor button while avoiding eye contact with Jake.

Jake was back in his office, sitting at his desk when it occurred to him that he had left his notepad in the football coach's office. He muttered a mild curse under his breath; he was hoping to get a jump on the football promotion plan that night. There was nothing he could do but take a detour to Slim's office on his way out and retrieve it.

He was walking down the cavernous corridor under the football stands, approaching the football offices, when Jake heard an angry, raised voice. It was Slim Haskins, saying, "You damn well better deliver the message, sweetie. And he better play ball with me on this, or you'll both find yourselves in more trouble than you ever imagined."

There was what sounded like a brief scuffle, a rustling sound like Slim was grabbing at someone who had pulled away from him. Instinctively, Jake stepped into the shadow of a large support pillar. A few moments later, a quietly sobbing Jennifer Stewart walked by. Thanks to the dim lighting, the shadow of the support pillar and Jennifer's state of mind, she passed by Jake as if he wasn't there.

Chapter Four

Jennifer Stewart went back to her office right after being confronted by Slim Haskins, sat at her desk in the dark and wept. It was obvious that Harvey's career and marriage were in jeopardy and she was caught in the middle. After crying uncontrollably for a few minutes, she regained control of her emotions and started to think of a plan. The best thing to do was talk to Harvey as soon as possible. But she needed to be smart about it. Jennifer typed a short note that said, "Harvey, just a reminder about your lunch meeting tomorrow, 1 p.m. at Charlie Parker's Diner on North Street. It is urgent - you absolutely must be there."

Charlie Parker's Diner was miles off campus and on the opposite side of the city from Harvey's house. There would be little chance that his wife or anyone from the university would stumble on them. It was an unnecessary precaution. Harvey was very well known in the area, but Jennifer was his assistant and she and Harvey having lunch together would probably not raise any eyebrows. Even so, Jennifer thought it wouldn't hurt to be extra careful.

She signed the note, laid it on Harvey's keyboard and left the athletic department building, choosing a route that took her farthest from the football offices. When she got to her apartment she collapsed on her sofa and cried again for an hour.

In the morning, Jake had his first meeting with a reporter from the local media. John Rose was the lead reporter for the sports department at the *State Journal-Register*, the daily newspaper in the city. Rose used the small amount of authority he had to assign himself to the Lincoln State major sports like men's football and basketball. The second-ranking sports reporter covered most of the women's sports and second-tier LSU sports like gymnastics. After the Lincoln State sports were assigned, all that was left for the third reporter on staff were high school sports, the Springfield Cardinals minor league baseball team and monitoring recreational softball league scores.

"Big Johnny" Rose (as he was known when he played football at Lincoln State, since he was six-feet-six and just short of three-hundred pounds) attended college at the same time as Jake and they had pretty much the same circle of friends while in school. They were good friends in college but had lost track of one another when Jake joined the service.

Jake walked into the Starbucks off-campus where they had agreed to meet and saw John waiting for him. Instead of a greeting, the first thing Rose said to Jake was, "So you must have survived that big scene at the athletic department office this morning!"

"What scene?" Jake asked, "I didn't go into the office this morning, I came right over here."

"One of the football players, a guy by the name of," John Rose consulted his notebook; "...Durrell Moore...crashed into the athletic office at 8 a.m. and pitched a fit. They had to call campus police to haul him away."

"How in the hell do you know about something that just happened a half hour ago?"

"My girlfriend is best friends with Marie, the receptionist. Marie had a front row seat for the whole show; in fact she was the one who called the cops, then she called me. As I understand it, this kid Durrell Moore was supposed to spend his upcoming junior year sitting on the bench for the football team. But he got a call a few weeks ago telling him the university took away his scholarship."

"That's too bad, but you and I both know athletes flunk out a lot. They need to maintain a 2.0 grade point average to keep their scholarship. Some of them don't do it."

"Grades weren't the problem in his case. This kid had a 3.5 GPA and no disciplinary or legal problems. It seems that Slim Haskins decided he wanted to make room for another player. In other words, Slim went over the maximum on his available scholarships and someone had to go. Durrell Moore apparently drew the short straw."

"Christ, I never heard of that happening. The poor kid; no wonder he was pissed off."

"It's called *oversigning*. Coming out of high school, when a college recruits an athlete, the kid assumes they have a four-year scholarship. That isn't true and it never has been. All scholarships have always been for one year only. There used to be an unwritten understanding that it was a four year deal, as long as the athlete kept decent grades and didn't have any disciplinary or legal problems. These days more coaches are kicking kids off scholarship, not for academics or disciplinary reasons, but because they realize that the kid isn't going to contribute much to the program. They dump the kid after a couple of years to make room for a shiny-faced freshman with the potential to be a star."

"Wow," Jake said, "how are you going to handle this in the paper?"

"I won't keep it under wraps but it doesn't necessarily belong on the front page either. I'll write my column tomorrow to focus on the problem of oversigning and bring up Durrell Moore as an example. I would obviously never print this, but it was a shitty thing for Slim Haskins to wait until right before the school term started to tell the kid. Now Durrell Moore either has to pay full tuition to attend school here or sit out a semester. From what I heard his family doesn't have much dough, so the kid is out of luck."

With the big news of the day already discussed, the rest of

the meeting went smoothly. Jake provided some human interest background on a couple of players and gave John plenty of optimistic quotes about the team's chances during the upcoming season.

Like most local sports reporters, John had a strange relationship with the Lincoln State sports teams. On one hand, he needed to come up with interesting stories and report anything that was newsworthy, whether it was good or bad. On the other hand, he depended on a handful of coaches, players and athletic department personnel to provide information to him. If he got on the wrong side of a few key people, their response would be to deny him access to what was going on in their sport. He would get no quotes, no inside information and he would be ignored by coaches and players alike at press conferences. If John were cut off from that information, he may as well go to work for *Good Housekeeping*. It was a fine line he had to walk, and John Rose did it as well or better than most reporters.

Harvey stood up from his desk; it was nearly 1 p.m. and he had to leave for his lunch meeting with Jennifer. Of course, his wife Sheila chose that moment to drop by unexpectedly. Jennifer was still in the front reception area, waiting for Harvey's other assistant to come back from lunch so she could leave. She stopped Sheila.

"Mrs. Elwood, Harvey is just getting ready to leave for a lunch appointment."

"Don't worry, my dear. I just need a moment of his time," Sheila said as she blew by Jennifer's desk and burst into Harvey's office. "Harvey! I thought you were calling the landscapers to reschedule fertilizing the garden. I have important guests coming later this afternoon and now the patio smells like cow dung."

"I forgot, Sheila. Believe it or not I have a lot on my mind. You could have called them, you know."

"I told you to do it. Did you forget? Do I have to worry about you having brain damage from all that head knocking you did when you played football back in the old days? I read about it in *People* magazine. Some retired players are considering a lawsuit against the NFL. You should look into that."

Leave it to Sheila, Harvey thought, to make it all about her. She was the most self-centered woman on the planet. And she was always looking to jump onto a legal bandwagon if it could provide more cash to support her lifestyle. It was hard to believe she came from a lower-middle class family and that her dad was a postal worker. She won the life lottery when she latched onto Harvey, but she tried to play the role of someone who had been born into tremendous wealth.

"I'm on my way out the door, Sheila. So long. Have fun with your party or whatever the hell it is."

Harvey walked quickly past Sheila and out of his office. He and Jennifer had agreed to take separate cars to meet for lunch.

There were only a handful of customers left in the diner when Harvey and Jennifer sat down. There wasn't a living soul within thirty feet of their corner booth.

"So tell me word for word what he said," Harvey instructed Jennifer after she had laid out the basics.

"Haskins called upstairs and asked me to deliver some papers, he said he needed them right away. I think he knew it would take awhile to gather what he wanted and it would be after everyone left before I got to the football offices. When I got there, he pulled out his cell phone and showed me a photo. It was of us in the boathouse. I think we were both too distracted at that moment to notice the flash."

Harvey ignored Jennifer's attempt at humor, "Is there any question from looking at the photo...?"

"You would have to be blind to not see what was happening in the picture. Both of our faces are definitely recognizable. I think Slim Haskins missed his career calling; he's a better photographer than football coach."

"Let's try to focus here, Jennifer. So what did he say then?"

"He said he will go public about us and ruin your career and your marriage if you don't renew his contract. A minimum of four more years is what he said. He also said to tell you he would give you a break and wouldn't demand a raise."

"The Athletic Board and Board of Trustees will never go along with renewing his contract. He's all but fired already. A conference championship might save him, but even that isn't a sure thing."

"His exact words were that you had better use all your charm to persuade them. Or else."

"Jesus Christ. Talk about being between a rock and a hard place. If I ask the board to renew his contract they'll fire me for being an idiot. If I don't do what he says, they'll fire me for having an affair with a student and I'll be ruined." Harvey put his head in his hands.

Jennifer's heart ached. She knew her affair with Harvey could blow up and lead to huge trouble, but naively she thought it would never happen. They had been so very discrete. Even though it started as a fun little fling, over the past eighteen months, she had grown to love Harvey. Not that she ever expected – or even wanted – it to be more than it was. She knew she would be OK, a few weeks after the articles appeared about her being a home-wrecking slut, people would move onto some other salacious story. In today's world, women actually came out of these things mostly unscathed and sometimes as minor celebrities. It would be Harvey's life that would be left in ruins. Her eyes began to fill with tears at the thought.

Harvey was outlining a plan to Jennifer. "I think the best thing to do is stall Haskins as long as we can. Ignore him for now. Maybe – and I know this is probably wishful thinking – the goddamn football team will win the first few games and take the heat off of Haskins for a while. If they don't start strong, I'm willing to bet he will approach you or hopefully will come directly me. I'm going to pick up a couple of miniature voice recorders. If he contacts me, I'll record him and you should also have a mini-recorder so you can do the same. We just may be able to turn the tables on that bastard."

Chapter Five

Two weeks passed uneventfully. After his altercation with Jennifer, Slim Haskins decided to let his demands simmer for a while and give her some time to work on Harvey. He felt no particular sense of urgency at the moment; he knew the Athletic Board wasn't going to fire him after one game. And with the opening game coming up on Saturday, he had plenty to do getting the team prepared.

The same afternoon he and Jennifer met for lunch, Harvey bought two tiny pocket voice recorders. He kept his recorder in his pocket and instructed Jennifer to keep her recorder in reach at all times. "Slim being the weasel that he is," he cautioned Jennifer, "he'll try to surprise you again like he did the last time. So be ready."

Jake had a busy two weeks and managed to get the pre-season publicity machine going full steam for the football season. His hard work seemed to be paying off – ticket sales had picked up during the past week and Jake was projecting attendance of at least 21,000 in the 27,000-seat stadium for the home opener against the Mid-Central University Cardinals. That would be an increase over the previous year's first home game.

In the past, it would be unusual for Lincoln State to play their first game of the season against a conference opponent like Mid-Central University. Until recent years, almost all college teams played three or four non-conference games before starting the conference schedule. Non-conference games counted in a team's record, but conference games were generally more important, so non-conference games were often used as a tune-up.

However, like all Athletic Directors of smaller schools, Harvey had figured out a few years ago that the athletic program made considerably more money by playing all of its non-conference games on the road, and he could further maximize the school's profit by keeping one or two dates open later in the season to accommodate non-conference games with major, big-name schools. That meant adjusting the schedule accordingly.

Harvey presented his idea to the Athletic Board. He said, "When Lincoln State plays a home football game, the average ticket sells for about $20 and we get a crowd of 20,000. Deduct all the costs of hosting a home game and we clear around $200,000. The teams in major conferences like the

Southeast, Big Ten and Pac Ten sell out their huge stadiums that hold 80,000 or even 100,000 fans, and they charge upwards of $40 a ticket. Do the math...big schools can guarantee Lincoln State a bigger payday for playing on the road than at home. Some of the powerful schools like University of Michigan are guaranteeing a million dollars for one game to teams like Lincoln State!"

With visions of million-dollar paydays rattling around in their heads, the Athletic Board gave Harvey free reign to schedule games with the primary goal of maximizing revenue. If that meant the Abes played three straight road games against vastly superior competition and took three straight beatings, it was for the greater good of the Lincoln State athletic department. This season's schedule had the first game at home, and then the Abes would hit the road for three straight weeks against Michigan State, UCLA and Tennessee. Those three opponents were all ranked among the top twenty-five teams in the nation. Then, instead of a much-welcomed week off in early November, the team would head south to play against the University of Florida. The Florida Gators were projected to contend for the national championship and would be eager to run up the score against a lesser opponent like Lincoln State. It could very well be a bloodbath.

A similar situation happened in basketball. Steve Jefferies kept Harvey from getting completely out of control with the basketball schedule, arguing that excessive travel for road games would destroy any chance of his players attending class on a regular basis. Still, the men's basketball team would be playing eight straight non-conference road games during December. Players would be subjected to nearly three straight weeks of brutal travel right before the start of final exams. Out of thirty basketball games on their schedule, Lincoln State men's basketball would host only ten home games during the upcoming season.

Jake Goodman's phone rang late Thursday afternoon. It was reporter John Rose, with some surprising news.

"Hey buddy! Guess where Maurice Jones, the starting quarterback for the Mid-Central Cardinals is sitting right now?"

"How should I know, Johnny. Sitting on the toilet?"

"Good guess, but wrong. He is at this moment sitting in a jail cell in Kentucky. He was caught breaking into some student's apartment last night. When the cops found him he was carrying a laptop computer that wasn't his and also stolen credit cards, not to mention an ounce of marijuana. Then for good measure he punched a cop while they were handcuffing him."

"Holy cow, how did you find out about this?"

"I just got a call from your counterpart at Mid-Central. I've done some favors for him in the past. He told me Maurice Jones is suspended for this week's game, probably longer unless some miracle happens and he's proven innocent."

"That's incredible news. If I recall, Jones is a senior and projected to be All-Conference, maybe even All-American. He's a great player. We were ten-point underdogs, but I think we stand a chance to win if he doesn't play."

"I know...it changes the whole game. Well, I'm going to let you spread the good news around your place. The first thing I would do is call Harvey, then let Haskins know. You'll look like a genius and it never hurts a guy in your position to be the bearer of glad tidings."

"Thanks Johnny. I owe you a big one."

"You got that right." With that Johnny hung up.

Jake immediately dialed Harvey's direct line and gave him the news. Harvey was ecstatic. When Jake asked if he should call Haskins or if Harvey wanted to deliver the news to Slim personally, Harvey told Jake to break the news to the football coach.

The game on Saturday turned out to be a good one for the Abes. The second-string quarterback for the Cardinals had no previous game experience. With two days to get ready for his first start he was woefully unprepared. Lincoln State took advantage of the opposing quarterback's inexperience to carry a 20-0 lead into the fourth quarter. Mid-Central mounted a comeback, but it was too little, too late and the Abes won the game 23-14.

Saturday was a beautiful September day, bright and sunny with temperatures in the low 70s. The good weather brought out a couple thousand fair-weather fans who bought tickets on game day. The paid attendance was announced at 24,610, the biggest crowd for an Abes football game in over four years.

On Monday, Jake had a scheduled meeting with Harvey to

update him on the progress of public relations for the fall sports. Harvey was in a joyful mood after the win on Saturday and the surprisingly good attendance. Harvey greeted Jake with a big smile and hard slap on the back, "My man! You did a great job – we haven't seen a crowd that big, not to mention that enthusiastic, in quite a while."

"I don't think I should take all the credit, Harvey. The news about Maurice Jones being out of the game built a lot of interest in the game and the nice weather certainly didn't hurt attendance."

"Don't be so modest. In this business, whenever someone gives you credit for something good, take every bit of it. Believe me; you'll have plenty of chances to accept blame when things go to shit, which they always do."

"Thank you, Harvey. I've made some good progress in promoting the other fall sports as well." Jake pulled out a summary of his promotional plan and went over it line by line with the Athletic Director.

"Your plans look excellent, Jake, just great. I knew you would be a success in this job and you haven't proved me wrong."

With their business settled Jake asked, "What do you think about the Maurice Jones situation? Do you think Mid-Central handled it correctly?"

"That's a tough call. Basically, they handed us that win on a silver platter by suspending Jones. But their hands were pretty much tied. Every school has a set of rules on how to handle those types of situations. My guess is that the Athletic Director and football coach at Mid-Central spent hours talking to the police, reading the police report and doing their own investigation. That's what I would have done. If they suspended Jones, I'm sure it was because the investigation confirmed the police version of things. They probably tried everything possible to make sure the player wasn't unfairly accused."

"Plus this would eventually become an NCAA matter if the school didn't take action."

"You're right. All member schools are bound by the National Collegiate Athletic Association rules, which are complicated, written in legalize and fill a very thick book. The NCAA allows the school some discretion in handling problems like this themselves. But if Mid-Central had let it slide and not punished Maurice Jones, the NCAA would have done its own investigation and then the whole athletic program may have been be punished."

"Has Lincoln State had any run-ins with the NCAA?"

"It's hard to avoid them. Try to understand what we're up against. Between the men's and women's teams, we have over three hundred student-athletes. Most of the students are short on cash, even with their scholarships. So the temptation is there. One of the biggest problems is the boosters; they are avid fans that want us to win so badly they do all kinds of stuff that's against the rules. You wouldn't believe the things I've seen boosters do over the years. A booster might give a player a 'golden handshake,' and slip him a couple hundred bucks. It used to be a common trick for local businesses to hire players for jobs and pay them even when they didn't show up. Businesses will give players free stuff. Take a restaurant owner who thinks he's doing nothing wrong when he lets a player eat for free. That's a violation. Other boosters will feel sorry for a player's family who can't afford to come to games and pay for their transportation and hotels. All of those things are against the rules and can get us punished even though the school has nothing to do with what happened. It's almost impossible to communicate hundreds of pages of complicated rules to college kids and boosters."

"That seems like a nightmare to deal with."

"You got that right. On top of that, any player who looks like he is a pro prospect will attract agents like raw meat attracts flies. Some of those agents can be real slime balls; they'll do anything to get a kid to sign with them, even if it means breaking the rules. If the agent gets caught, it usually isn't the agent who suffers, but the kid may lose his eligibility and Lincoln State gets punished."

"Lincoln State has had a pretty good track record of staying out of trouble, at least I haven't seen much in the news."

"We've done pretty well, other than football. We rely a lot on the coaches since they are the ones who are closest to the players. Take Steve Jefferies. He has never had a hint of a problem with rule violations on the basketball team. I think it's because he follows up on any potential problems before they turn into real situations. Steve and I spoke a few weeks ago. One of his players comes to campus at the end of summer driving a new SUV. Of course, Steve asks the kid how he got it, to make sure it wasn't a gift from some booster. The player tells Steve he saved for the down payment from his summer job and got a bank loan for the rest. Steve made the kid's parents produce the sale receipt, loan agreement that the parents co-signed, even stubs from the kid's summer paychecks. He doesn't let his players bullshit him."

Jake asked, "What about football?"

"That's been a bit of a problem area, but still not as bad as some other schools. I know Haskins has his hands full with close to a hundred players. But he doesn't make a personal effort to stay on top his players about the rules. Our Compliance Officer does a two-hour presentation at the beginning of the year, hands out an NCAA rule book and that's all the education about it that the football players get. As a result, small violations have turned into bigger problems and we've had a few touchy situations with the NCAA over the past several years. Nothing fatal, but a few players have been suspended."

"Can I ask you a question that's really none of my business? What are the chances Slim Haskins will be around next season?"

Harvey's face reddened and he seemed to measure his words carefully before he answered, "It depends on the rest of the season, Jake. Last Saturday didn't hurt his chances and expectations aren't very high. As the Athletic Director, I try to do everything I can to keep the football program running smoothly. That means not making a coaching change unless there is a compelling reason to do so. As much as it pains me to say this, I will stand behind Slim Haskins until the situation indicates otherwise."

Jake walked out of the meeting somewhat confused by Harvey's sudden show of support for the football coach. Two "compelling reasons" to fire Haskins could be the total of five wins by the Abes over the past two seasons and the history of NCAA violations. One win against a team missing their star quarterback didn't seem like enough of a turnaround to make Harvey into a Slim Haskins fan overnight.

Chapter Six

Slim Haskins stared at the blank wall in the office of the visiting team locker room at Spartan Stadium. In thirty years in coaching, he had never experienced a worse press conference than the one he just endured. He walked off the field thinking the Abes had made a good showing, losing to Michigan State by a score of 29-21. They had been within a touchdown late in the third quarter, playing against a nationally ranked team on their home field. The Vegas betting line had Michigan State as a twenty point favorite, for crying out loud.

Yet what did the reporters all seem to want to talk about at the post-game press conference? They all wanted to know whether Slim was worried about his job. He had tried to deflect the questions, first with humor, then by changing the subject, and then by giving short, irritated answers. But those fucking reporters just kept on pushing. Finally Slim had enough and blew a gasket in front of twenty reporters, not to mention a number of TV cameras and radio microphones. He launched into a two-minute, obscenity-laced tirade that would make the most calloused sailor cringe.

This unfortunate event would certainly be a big story in Central Illinois, probably throughout the Midwest, and maybe even nationally. What should have been at least a fairly positive day had turned into a nightmare.

Sitting alone in the front row on the six-hour bus ride to Springfield, the coach couldn't help looking back at his coaching career, which looked like it could be nearing an end. He had played linebacker in college but wasn't a standout by any measure. What he did have was the ability to lead his fellow teammates and also possessed what coaches call a good "football mind." He made the decision even before his playing days were over that he would pursue coaching as a career.

After graduation, Donald Haskins (he hadn't picked up the "Slim" nickname yet) enrolled in graduate school at the University of Nebraska and applied for a position as a part-time assistant coach. It was a very low-paying position but was perfect for a twenty-three year old aspiring to a coaching career. At that time, Nebraska was a national power and the coaching staff was packed with talented assistants who went on to be successful head coaches throughout the nation. Young Donald Haskins kept his mouth closed and his ears open and soaked up not only coaching know-how but the aura of a successful program.

As Slim gazed out the bus window and reminisced, he decided it wasn't worth the mental effort to count the seasons he spent as an assistant. Many of those seasons were at low pay and he relocated every few years, which didn't matter to him since football consumed so much of his life that there was no room for women or marriage or family.

Finally, nearly two decades of toiling as an assistant coach paid off and Slim landed a head coaching job at a Division I football program at the age of forty. He spent seven years there with results that were good but not great. His performance was good enough to keep him employed for seven years, over twice the average for a head coach in Division I college football. The turnover of head coaches in Division I is very high; for example, in the thirteen-team Mid-American Conference during the past decade, the average head coach lasted little more than two years and there were 25 head coaching changes. Of the 120 coaches in Division I college football in 2010, only 36 held their position for over five years.

Like every stop he made in his coaching career, Slim's abrasive personality wore thin and he was dismissed. Fortunately, two years remained on his contract and he received a six figure buy-out – not enough money to retire, but he could live comfortably while he looked for another head coaching spot. During three decades in coaching, Slim made many contacts in the world of college sports and one was Harvey Elwood at Lincoln State. He landed an interview for the open coaching slot and got the job.

Now it looked like his coaching career was over, or at least his days as a head coach. Only about nineteen head coaching jobs opened up in Division I football each year. Each Division I team had about ten assistant coaches, so there were over a thousand young up-and-comers trying to scramble up the coaching ladder at any given time. Many of them chased after the nineteen yearly head coach openings.

Nobody recognized more than Slim that his recent record at Lincoln State, not to mention his age and volatile personality, would keep him from being hired as a head coach somewhere else. He knew that his only hope to stay in head coaching was to keep his job at Lincoln State.

When the bus pulled into the parking lot at Lincoln State, Slim had already decided that it was time to turn up the heat on Jennifer Stewart and Harvey Elwood.

Harvey Elwood was not having the best Saturday night either. He had passed up an opportunity to travel with the football team in the hope that he and Jennifer would be able to spend a few hours together. But his wife Sheila had other plans. She arranged for her and Harvey to host a dinner party at Sebastian's Hideout restaurant in downtown Springfield for three other couples.

Although Harvey tried to be a gracious host, he found his thoughts constantly drifting to Jennifer. He was quiet and distant throughout the evening. As he drove home, Sheila chided him about his behavior.

"What's your problem, Harvey? You acted like that dinner was the last place you wanted to be."

"This hasn't been a very good day. I spent two hours on the

phone this afternoon with reporters and then another half-hour with Jake Goodman outlining our plan for disarming the situation. You may have heard my phone ring twice during dinner – those were Athletic Board members. And they were not happy."

"Don't they realize it's a Saturday night and you have social plans? You should have been polite to our guests and just turned off your phone."

I would rather be screamed at by a board member than talk to those people you invited to dinner, Sheila. Where do you dig up these losers?"

"If you would have been paying attention this evening you would know that Gerald Dunkelberg served as Second Assistant Ambassador to the country of Uruguay for five years!"

Harvey couldn't help but laugh, "Which one was he, the guy with the bow tie? I would have asked for his autograph had I known that."

"Not everyone interesting has to be a jock-strap, you know."

Sheila thought Harvey hated that term and took it as an insult, but actually Harvey found it annoying that she never could remember that it was just "jock." Christ, she was stupid.

"You know, Harvey, you've been acting like even more of a prick than usual lately. And you know, I do notice when you disappear to a mysterious meetings for a few hours once or twice a week. I'm not stupid – I also see the way that girl who works in your office looks at you. What is her name?

Jennifer something?"

Harvey had been around this block before and his face didn't show a bit of emotion. He responded, "Sheila, I'm too busy to have an affair. Just like you've been too busy for the past ten years to have sex more than once every two months." Sheila's frigidity had been a constant focus of arguments between them over the years. In the past few years, Harvey finally gave up trying to change her and discretely sought sexual companionship elsewhere.

"You used to try, Harvey; you don't even bother to do that anymore."

Harvey could think of nothing else to say. He was silent the rest of the ride home, thinking how he could work a couple of visits to Jennifer into his schedule this week.

Unlike Harvey and Slim Haskins, Jake Goodman was having a very pleasant Saturday night. Earlier in the week, he stopped in the coffee room of the athletic office and introduced himself to one of the administrative assistants. Ellen Benjamin caught Jake's eye a few times as he walked through the second floor cubicle farm. She had dark hair that framed her tan face and showed off gorgeous brown eyes, and a tall frame that was at the same time muscular but very feminine. She was an All-American soccer player at the University of Illinois in her college days and still was a star player in amateur leagues around the area. After a few minutes of small talk, Jake asked her out and during the past few hours learned that Ellen had a sparkling intelligence and sense of humor that he really enjoyed.

When Jake picked Ellen up, they spoke briefly about the Lincoln State loss and Slim Haskins' meltdown at the press conference. After Jake got off the phone with Harvey immediately after the game, Jake hammered the phones hard trying to do damage control with the Springfield area press. He excused himself from dinner with Ellen once in order to talk to Johnny Rose, who wanted a quote from Jake about the situation. But other than that, they had tried to ignore the topic.

Now on the way home from dinner, Ellen said, "Do you think this crisis with Slim Haskins will blow over or is he finished?"

"I'm pretty sure it will blow over. It doesn't happen often that a coach goes crazy like that, but it isn't the first time and won't be the last time. I don't know that Slim Haskins will be kept on after the season ends, but there's really nothing to be gained by firing him after two games."

"I'm sure this will be all over the local news, it'll probably even make ESPN."

"Yeah, it probably will. But in a day or two someone else in sports will act like an ass and the media will latch onto that. It will blow over."

"It'll be interesting to see what happens," Ellen said as Jake pulled to the front of her apartment building, "hey, do you want to come up to my place and watch some ESPN?"

***

Jake's assessment of the situation was correct. The storm

surrounding Slim Haskins did fade away. As usual, the Saturday night sports broadcasts in Central Illinois did not ignore the football coach's outburst at the press conference, but the focus of the coverage was the surprisingly strong showing by the Abes. Keeping the game close against a highly ranked school like Michigan State was the main story and the outrageous behavior of Slim Haskins was the sideshow.

Harvey summoned Jake to his office on Monday morning. "It looks like our plan for damage control worked out, Jake. Things could have been a lot worse."

"Thanks for the advice on that, Harvey, I appreciate it. We were lucky that the game gave everyone something else to focus on."

"I saw last night that ESPN was still playing the clip where Slim told that young female reporter that what she really needed was a good screwing," Harvey said with a laugh.

"Slim will go down as one of the biggest douche bag coaches ever."

"He handled this whole thing terribly, no question about it, and he is walking on thin ice. But as Athletic Director I have to look at the way we played Saturday. I'm starting to think that this season may turn into something special and I'm not going to fire Slim Haskins after two games for being a jerk."

Thursday was a blustery late summer day, rainy and windy. Jennifer Stewart slipped on her coat and headed out the door for a quick lunch and a few errands. As she walked out, she patted her pocket to make sure she had the tiny voice recorder that Harvey gave her. Earlier in the week Harvey visited her apartment, the first time they had been able to spend time together in over a week. As he kissed her goodbye, he reminded her to keep the recorder with her at all times. "After what happened this weekend, Haskins is feeling insecure. He may approach one of us this week," Harvey said.

***

Jennifer had just hit the remote to unlock her car doors when Slim Haskins appeared seemingly from nowhere. He must have been hiding alongside the car next to hers, Jennifer thought. She subtly reached into her pocket and turned on the recorder.

"What do you want?" she said rudely.

"And a fine good morning to you on this beautiful day," Haskins said sarcastically as he moved so close to her that his face was inches from hers.

"I have things to do. Like I said, what do you want?"

"What I want is for you to tell me some good news. We haven't talked for a few weeks. What's the answer?"

"I don't know. Harvey hasn't made up his mind."

"Today is Thursday. By one week from today I expect something," and with that Haskins turned and walked away.

Shaking, Jennifer got into her car. She turned off the voice recorder, rewound it to the start of the message and hit the play button. It certainly didn't sound like a friendly conversation, but it was hardly evidence of blackmail. Did Haskins purposely choose his words to avoid incriminating himself? Or was it simply bad luck that he said absolutely nothing that made him guilty of anything?

Chapter 7

The next football game was at UCLA, the big "travel game" of the early season. Like many Athletic Directors, Harvey scheduled at least one away game each season in a warm weather location. This year the Abes were traveling to Southern California. The key people in the athletic department were all making the trip, as well as a few thousand alumni and Lincoln State fans.

The team traveled to California a day earlier than usual to give the players some time to enjoy the sun. Road trips like this were a carrot that the football coaching staff dangled in front of potential recruits to sway them to sign with Lincoln State and the players usually had them highlighted on their schedules. The coaches enjoyed the trips but also faced an extra burden of keeping the players focused for the game. It was a lot easier to focus on football when the players were at a Holiday Inn in Akron than it was at a resort in Los Angeles.

The rest of the athletic administration staff were flying to L.A. on Friday and returning Sunday evening with the team. There was a reception and pep rally scheduled late Friday afternoon in a rented ballroom at the team hotel. Fans and alumni could part with $50 per person for the privilege of eating hotel buffet food and rubbing elbows for a couple of hours with coaches, players, cheerleaders and athletic department staffers.

Jake was looking forward to the trip. UCLA played their home games in the Rose Bowl, one of the most historic and famous stadiums in the nation. It wouldn't be a vacation for him; he was the informal host to about a dozen members of the media who made the journey from Illinois. Even with the work involved, Jake thought, it would be a welcome change to spend a few days in the sun and away from the office.

Because they were returning Sunday on the team charter, Jake and most of the other athletic department staffers boarded a one-way commercial flight to Los Angeles Friday morning. Molly was in charge of the Friday afternoon reception so she flew out Thursday, accompanied by Jennifer Stewart. Harvey insisted that Molly have someone help her coordinate the event and suggested Jennifer Stewart would be a good choice. Everything had been arranged in advance weeks ahead of time, but Molly welcomed the extra help in dealing with the last minute details.

Lincoln State used the "travel game" as a perk and allowed coaches and staffers to bring their families, so many spouses were traveling to California. Sheila Elwood had other plans for the weekend and Harvey didn't try to persuade her to make the trip. It had been a quiet and sullen week in the Elwood house and Harvey was looking forward to getting away. Ellen made a vague overture to Jake about making the trip with him, but he gingerly discouraged her. He liked Ellen but didn't want things to move anywhere near that fast.

The first thing that struck Jake as he boarded the plane was the preponderance of royal blue and gray. It looked like many of the fans attending the game had booked this flight.

Jake took his seat and saw that he was sharing his row with Milt Atkins and his wife. Jake had spoken briefly with Milt a couple of times over the past few weeks but hadn't worked closely with him like he had with Molly on the women's side of the department. Harvey confided in Jake one day, "Milt is a bumbling idiot. It isn't that he's a bad guy; he's just lousy at his job. Milt got hired before I took over as Athletic Director. He was buddies with a couple of the board members and still is. I'm stuck with him, so all I can do is make sure he doesn't do any damage. I try to do all the important stuff and leave what's left to Milt."

Milt Atkins thrust out his right hand. "Jake Goodman! Glad to have you with us for the trip. This is my wife Susan," he said as he nodded toward the woman sitting in the window seat. Susan Atkins turned toward Jake and nodded, as if it took a supreme effort to acknowledge him.

"Good to meet you, Susan. I'm glad we're sitting together, Milt, we haven't had much of a chance to talk," Jake said diplomatically.

"Right, I don't get too involved in the promotion and sports information side of things. I mostly handle administrative matters."

Jake looked at Milt and couldn't help but think of Deputy Barney Fife from the old TV show. Milt was slightly built, maybe five-foot-eight inches tall and one-hundred-thirty pounds. He was dressed in a loud, royal blue and gray checked sport coat that had to be custom-made, Jake thought, because no self-respecting clothing store would dare to have such a hideous jacket hanging on their rack. He wore a royal blue shirt and a tie with a pattern of tiny Abes logos.

"That's quite an outfit you have on, Milt," Jake said jokingly.

"Didn't you get Harvey's memo saying there would be lots of fans on this flight so we should dress appropriately?"

"I did get the memo, that's why I'm wearing this," Jake said as he pointed to his own gray sweater with a subtle royal blue Abes logo on the right breast.

"Over the years I've accumulated more than my share of Lincoln State fan-wear. I'm a proud Abe, you know, class of '81. One of my favorite things about a trip like this is that we get to show our school pride. We aren't one of the big boys like UCLA, but we do have the Springfield spirit!"

Jake looked past Milt and caught Susan rolling her eyes. She met Jake's glance briefly and then quickly found something interesting to look at outside the plane window.

With a personality to match his flamboyant outfit, Milt

turned out to be an entertaining seat-mate, especially after the flight attendant served him a couple of double martinis. Even Susan cheered up after she downed a couple of drinks. With the many fans on board and possibly within earshot, no business was discussed on the flight.

The reception and pep rally went smoothly and was the start of a wonderful weekend for Lincoln State and its fans. Jake lingered after the reception and was chatting with Harvey when Molly and Jennifer came to join them.

"Hey you guys," Molly said enthusiastically, "this thing turned out to be great, didn't it? Everyone had a good time and we ended up making about forty-grand on this little fundraiser!"

"Good deal," Harvey said with a smile and raised his glass toward Molly and Jennifer, "you two did a fantastic job. I tell you what, dinner is on me tonight."

"Actually I made plans to have dinner with an old classmate of mine who lives in the area now," Molly said.

"I don't have any plans, Mr. Elwood," Jennifer said, "and maybe Jake would like to join us."

He didn't consciously think about it at that moment, but weeks later Jake looked back and realized that something in Jennifer's tone, or maybe Harvey's expression, made him feel he really wasn't welcome at dinner. "I think I'll pass," Jake said, "I think I'll give Johnny Rose a call and see if he and some of the other reporters want to explore the L.A. night-life."

"A bunch of bachelors loose on the town," Harvey said, "I hope you guys stay out of trouble."

Jake called Johnny Rose, who had made plans with several other visiting Illinois reporters for a night out. They were glad to have Jake join them. No laws were broken but as Jake's head hit the pillow at 2 a.m. his last waking thought was that he was glad the game had a late afternoon start time.

The UCLA Bruins came on the field brimming with confidence that they would take an early lead and the small-school bumpkins from the Midwest would quickly roll over and give up. Unfortunately for the Bruins, the Abes were the ones who got off to a fast start.

On the first play from scrimmage, the UCLA quarterback dropped back to pass and was blindsided by Abes defensive end Onolulo Kahona. The ball popped free and was picked up by the Lincoln State nose guard, who rumbled in for a touchdown. On the ensuing kick-off, the shell-shocked Bruins stood like statues while the Abes executed a perfect onside kick. The very next play was a long pass to score again and put Lincoln State ahead by two touchdowns.

The rest of the game was not pretty, but it was effective for Lincoln State. Both teams had a difficult time on offense and the Abes led 14-9 entering the fourth quarter. UCLA drove down the field as the game clock wound down and had the ball at the six-yard-line with fifteen seconds left in the game. If UCLA scored a touchdown, it would be a second straight disappointing loss for the Abes.

Luckily for Lincoln State, Onolulo Kahona didn't learn very much about football growing up in American Samoa. He never heard the storied history of the UCLA Bruins and didn't know that the Rose Bowl was built in 1922 and hosted some of the most famous sporting events of the Twentieth Century. All he knew was that his beloved grandmother, his favorite person on the face of the planet, was sitting in the stands. She had come all the way from Samoa just to see him play this strange game she knew nothing about. More than anything in the universe, he wanted to impress her.

The monstrous Samoan garnered every bit of strength on the next play and ran over the huge UCLA left tackle like he wasn't there. The game ended the same way it started, with Onolulo Kahona slamming into the quarterback and knocking the ball loose. Another Lincoln State lineman fell on the ball as the clock ticked to zero.

The mood was so joyous that Lincoln State fans, coaches, football team and administrative staff almost could have flown home without an airplane. The charter jet with the team and staffers had a party-like atmosphere. Even Slim Haskins was in a buoyant mood on the flight back to Springfield.

On Sunday night at home, the football coach laid in his bed staring at the darkness. They won the game, a monumental upset. He certainly earned the right to coach the rest of the season; there would be no mid-season firing. But was this win enough to keep his job at the end of the year? If only he hadn't blown up at that press conference! He chastised himself – he'd been around the coaching game long enough to keep his cool in situations like that. And one game doesn't make up for the past two seasons that had a total of five wins. Anything short of an amazing record and his contract would likely not be renewed. The potential was there for a job-saving season, but right now might be the perfect opportunity to press his bet with Harvey. Harvey could justify the extension by using the big upset to convince the board, but it needed to happen quickly while everyone was still basking in the UCLA win. Haskins liked dealing with that girl Jennifer instead of Harvey; she was easily intimidated and apparently had great influence with the Athletic Director. Slim Haskins would pay Jennifer a visit, this time drop by her apartment where there was no chance he might be overheard.

The doorbell in Jennifer Stewart's apartment rang shortly after 8 p.m. Thursday night. "Who is it?" She asked on the intercom.

"Don Haskins, I need to talk to you. "

"I'm busy. Stop by my office tomorrow."

"I know you're alone. Harvey had to work late at the office. Don't worry, I'm not going to hurt you, I just want to talk and it's better for you if we do it in private. Would you rather talk about this in your cubicle and have someone overhear us, for Christ's sake?"

"Come on up," said Jennifer as she buzzed him in. She grabbed the mini-recorder, turned it on and slipped it in the breast pocket of her opened, button-down flannel shirt.

Slim Haskins walked in. Jennifer didn't offer him a chair. That was alright with him; he figured it would be better if he stayed standing. "I think the time is right for Harvey to talk to the board about my contract extension," he said.

Jennifer had been planning how to bait the trap for a week. She needed to get Haskins to spell out exactly what he wanted. "I want to you to tell me, what will you do if you don't get your contract extension?"

"Sweetie, you know what I'll do. I'll go straight to the Board of Trustees, and then to the media. I'll show them those pictures I have of you and Harvey going at it like a couple of stray cats."

"This is blackmail!"

"Call it whatever you want. Just do what I'm fucking telling you to do and sell him on the idea."

Suddenly, Jennifer became enraged. She had the upper hand now with Haskins confessing to blackmail on the recorder. She decided it was time to get in his face for a change. She moved close to him. "Now it's time to listen to me, you fat fuck. I'll talk to Harvey, but I wouldn't count on anything. You just might be surprised what's in store for you." With that Jennifer pulled her hand back to slap Haskins in the face.

His reactions took over and he grabbed Jennifer's forearm tightly with his left hand. His right hand began to ball into a fist but he managed to control his anger enough to stop himself from punching her. Instead he pushed her. Jennifer fell backwards and, as the rest of her body hit the floor, the back of her head struck the stone bottom of the fireplace. She was semi-conscious and very badly dazed. It looked like there was a fair amount of blood; she probably cut her head when she fell.

Slim paused a few moments to think. Now he was looking at being charged with battery if she went to the police. Panic began to engulf him. But wait! He still had the upper hand. As long as he had those pictures, she would keep her mouth shut. She would tell people it was an accident; she fell in her apartment. She would probably tell Harvey what happened, but that really didn't matter either, because Harvey's hands were also tied.

Just in case she does decide to file charges, he thought, better be careful and not leave evidence he was there. What had he touched in her apartment? He grabbed a handful of paper napkins and hastily wiped off anything he remembered touching. He couldn't resist bending over and making sure she was breathing. She seemed to be coming out of it. She was moaning quietly and seemed to be breathing all right.

He left Jennifer Stewart exactly where she fell and quietly walked out of her apartment, wiping the doorknob after he closed the door. He paused and decided to leave her apartment door unlocked. When Jennifer came to, she may call someone for assistance and they would need to get into her apartment. Thankfully, no one was in the hall when he walked to the front of the building. He stopped at the building entrance and quickly wiped the doorknob and call button. He looked around and saw no one, before walking to his car and driving slowly off.

Slim Haskins didn't notice Sheila Elwood slouched low behind the wheel of a Mercedes parked across the street.

Chapter Eight

"Where's Jennifer this morning?" Harvey asked his full-time assistant. Jennifer's chair was empty when he arrived to the office on Friday.

"It's Friday morning, so she should have been here at eight. Then she normally leaves for an eleven o'clock class," his assistant answered, "she hasn't called in sick or anything."

"Call her and see if she answers her cell phone," Harvey said. She probably overslept, he thought. Graduate assistants were not the most reliable workers and many college students believed the weekend started on Thursday night. Jennifer was better than the average grad assistant about showing up for work, but she was barely twenty-three and he knew from experience that she could act her age sometimes. If she didn't turn up by noon he would visit her apartment at lunch.

Molly Bennett stopped by Harvey's office to review the final numbers for the reception fund raiser held in California. One of Molly's assignments was to devise new and clever ways to separate boosters and alumni from their money; holding a reception and pep rally at the biggest travel football game of the season was her idea. Her first effort the previous football season barely broke even but this one appeared to have done significantly better. Molly was brimming with enthusiasm as she presented the final accounting of income and expenses to Harvey.

"Do you remember right after the reception when I told you I thought we hit forty thousand in profit?" Molly began, "Well, check this out. It looks like we cleared closer to forty-two thousand!"

"That's fantastic! You did a super job on this project, Molly. Any chance we can hold more than one of these events every year?"

"You read my mind. I think only one road football game, the big travel game. We're not going to duplicate this when we play in Akron or places like that. The big travel game is special. What I was thinking is that we can do this once or twice a year for home games. Charge forty bucks or so to get in, have the band and cheerleaders on hand to entertain, you can even give a little pep talk. Hold the event in the basketball arena or rope off the practice football field if the weather is nice. Make it an event."

"The only thing is, what about the local bars and restaurants around the stadium? There are only four or five home football games a year and they do a huge business on game days. If we draw two thousand people to our event, those businesses lose a lot of their customers."

"I know the numbers, Harvey. I've read the studies on the dollar impact of college football on the local economy; there is a ton of data on this subject. For a home game at Lincoln State, about half the fans are local and half travel from out of town. It's the fans who travel from outside Springfield that spend the most. The average traveling fan drops about a hundred and thirty bucks around town on food, gas, souvenirs, parking, and stuff like that. Most of that money is spent within a two-mile radius of the stadium. Local fans spend money too, but quite a bit less. You can figure about fifty bucks a game average per local fan. You add it all together and a home football game brings about $2.4 million dollars into local businesses. Four home games like this we're playing season results in about ten million dollars to the Springfield economy."

"If local area businesses think we're trying to take that away from them, I can just picture the hell they'll raise."

"Since when did you develop a conscience about stuff like this, Harvey? Two thousand times forty dollars is eighty thousand dollars, over fifty thousand in profit. Twice a year that brings us a hundred grand a year. That is suhweeeet!"

Budgets were lean in the athletic department and Molly had just come up with one hundred thousand reasons that convinced Harvey. "Do you think you'll have time to get one of these set up yet for this season? We still have three home games left. How about trying to hold one for our early November game against Tulsa?"

"I'll see what I can do. But here's the deal, Harvey. This is my baby and I think that women's sports should benefit from my effort. Unless you want to let Milt handle this project."

"Good God, Molly! That would be a disaster. All right, I'll make sure the lion's share of the money goes your way. But only as much as I can without raising eyebrows."

"It's a deal. I'll start setting up the logistics and work with Jake Goodman on promotion."

Molly left his office and Harvey looked worriedly at his watch. Throughout his meeting with Molly, Harvey occasionally glanced through his open office door to see if Jennifer had arrived. Now it was after eleven and she should be sitting in her class. Her Friday morning class was an economics lecture in the big classroom in Tracy Hall, if he wasn't mistaken. That was only a short walk from his office; he decided to peek in the lecture hall and see if he spotted Jennifer. If she wasn't in class he'd visit her apartment.

It was a beautiful fall day as Harvey walked the few minutes to Tracy Hall. With all the students lounging around outside enjoying the weather throwing flying discs or just sitting on the lawns relaxing, Harvey suspected that the classrooms must be nearly empty. Any more eighty-degree days would be a rarity with September nearly past and the students were taking full advantage. Good for them, Harvey thought, and wondered if Jennifer decided to take a day off.

The main lecture room in Tracy Hall was nearly full to its hundred-student capacity; it was an advanced economics class and apparently graduate students took life more seriously than underclassmen. Harvey stood in the back of the hall and slowly scanned the backs of heads, row by row. After about five minutes he determined that Jennifer was not present and he walked to his car, which was in the athletic department parking lot.

As Harvey turned onto the street where Jennifer's apartment building was located, blue and red flashing police car lights dominated the scene. Yellow crime scene tape was stretched across the pillars near the front entrance to her apartment building. Harvey's heart rose up into his throat; he had the feeling one gets when driving home and sees an ambulance or fire truck leaving their neighborhood with sirens blaring. His gut told him that there was something terribly wrong.

"What's going on here?" Harvey asked a patrol cop.

"Homicide," the cop answered sternly.

"Who was it? Someone who lived here?"

"Yeah, some co-ed. Hey, you're Harvey Elwood, aren't you?"

"Yes, I am. I stopped by to check on one of my department employees who didn't show up as scheduled for work today. She lives in this building."

"Then you had better speak to Detective Martin. If it turns out to be someone who you worked with, you may be able to help us in the investigation."

Eduardo Martin was early-forties, neatly cut dark hair, about five-ten, with a trim build and wearing a dark suit, white shirt and blue patterned tie. Martin looked very much the detective. He wasn't exactly Joe Friday, but to use street slang, Eduardo Martin "smelled like a cop." Around the station house, the other cops referred to Detective Martin as "Clean Eddie," a commentary on his appearance as well as his twenty-year, spotless record on the police force. Harvey found himself thinking that he never even realized Springfield had detectives on the police force.

"Hey, Detective Martin," the patrol cop called toward Eddie, "This is Harvey Elwood from the university. It's possible that he knows the victim."

Eduardo Martin walked casually toward Harvey and put out his hand. "Mr. Elwood, good to meet you. I'm a Lincoln State grad, class of eighty-eight. That UCLA game last week was a big thrill."

"Thanks, Detective Martin. I came by here checking on one of my assistants, Jennifer Stewart. She lives in this building and didn't show up for work today."

Harvey knew at that moment that it was Jennifer who was murdered. The detective's face flashed recognition and emotion for a brief second before he regained his composure.

"If I tell you this, it is with the understanding you will cooperate and keep this confidential until we contact the family. Ms. Stewart was found dead in her apartment this morning. There's an outside chance it was an accidental fall, but we're treating it as a homicide. Cause of death was head trauma."

Harvey tried to hide his emotions but his insides were churning and his head was spinning. He had so many questions. He asked, "How did the police find out?"

"Listen, Mr. Elwood. I can tell this is a shock to you. I've already told you more than I am supposed to. I'll answer your question but that's all you get. And like I said, you absolutely must keep our discussion confidential. We received an anonymous tip this morning, a male caller from a pay phone – Christ, I didn't even know there were any pay phones left in the city. We followed up and found Ms. Stewart."

"Thank you, detective. I won't say a word about this to anyone until I see it reported on the news."

"Sorry to meet you under these circumstances, Mr. Elwood," the detective paused, then asked, "Say, is it standard procedure for you to personally check on employees who don't come to work?"

Harvey thought quickly, "Usually not, but Jennifer Stewart was my personal assistant and working on a special project for me. That's why her absence was unusual enough for me to follow up."

That answer seemed to satisfy the detective, "I see. Again, I'm very sorry. Do you have a business card? I may have some follow-up questions."

They traded business cards and then Eddie Martin shook hands with Harvey and walked away.

Harvey couldn't bear to return to the office. He called his assistant to tell her he wasn't feeling well and was taking the rest of the day off. He felt like he was half-dazed. His state of shock was too deep for him to have a rational thought about who might have done this to Jennifer. He drove home on autopilot.

The Elwood house was bustling when Harvey walked in the door. He had forgotten: it was Sheila's turn to host her book club meeting today and her guests would be arriving shortly. Sheila was in an ebullient mood. With the help of the house-keeper, she was arranging chairs and setting up a table full of food.

"Harvey...you're home early my dear! Did you decide to take the afternoon off and enjoy the beautiful day?"

"No Sheila, I'm not feeling well. I'm going upstairs." He looked straight ahead and moved briskly to the stairs to avoid any further conversation. He closed the drapes tightly, dropped his clothes on the floor and got into bed. He stared at the dark wall and tried to shut out all thoughts of the past hour. Numbness engulfed his soul – his mind held nothing but shock and sorrow. The only conscious thought that crept into his brain was that he was somehow to blame for Jennifer's death.

Jennifer's murder was the lead story on the local evening news. Harvey's phone rang shortly before 4 p.m. but he didn't answer; he muted it. By the time he woke up two hours later there were over thirty messages. He didn't have the strength to listen to them; he held his phone far away from his ear and deleted them one-by-one before they even played.

Sheila's book club was long gone by the time Harvey woke

up. Of course, Sheila wanted to go out for dinner, but Harvey said he was staying in bed. "I'll sleep in one of the guest rooms," Sheila said, "I certainly don't want to catch your germs." That suited Harvey perfectly; he wanted no human contact tonight, least of all Sheila.

Ellen Benjamin called Jake as he was getting out of the shower. His first thought was she was calling about their date that evening. He picked up the phone and said, "Hi Ellen, what is it that couldn't wait forty-five minutes until I pick you up?"

"You haven't heard what happened, have you?" Ellen said, "I just saw on the evening news, Jennifer Stewart was found dead this morning...and they think it was murder."

"What? I can't believe it. What else did the news say?"

"Not much. Apparently head injuries, they think it happened last night. Nothing was stolen, didn't seem to be robbery or anything like that."

"That's sad. I didn't see her much around the office, but talked to her for a while a few weeks ago. She seemed like a nice girl."

Slim Haskins and his football squad just got off a plane in Knoxville, Tennessee when he heard the news about Jennifer. The Abes were playing the Tennessee Volunteers the following evening. One of his players approached him and held up his cell phone. "Coach, did you hear about the news on campus?"

"No, I've been too busy getting ready for the game. That's

what you should be doing too instead of farting around on your phone."

"Some grad student who works in the athletic office...they found her dead this morning."

The football coach's face turned ashen and his stomach went into a knot. "Who was it, did they say?"

"Let's see," the player looked at his phone, "it was somebody named Jennifer Stewart. She lived right off campus."

The knot in Slim's stomach began twisting violently. He fought to keep his composure and tried to keep his tone of voice casual. "Right near campus, huh? Did they arrest anyone? Or did they say they have a suspect?"

"Doesn't look like it, but I think this news just came out an hour or so ago. Are you all right coach? You look pale."

"I'm fine, just feeling a little bit airsick," Slim lied. He managed to get himself under control. He replayed the events of the previous night carefully in his mind; he played it back frame by frame like a video in super-slow motion. He went over every millisecond when he and Jennifer struggled and he pushed her down. He concluded that he did not push her that hard.

He would concede that Jennifer was definitely dazed when he left her apartment; there was no question about that. But he had checked her out; she was breathing evenly and already starting to regain her senses when he walked out the door. He'd seen dozens of head injuries over the years and knew the difference between one that was serious and someone who just got their bell rung.

Unlike Harvey, Slim didn't have the luxury of hiding out in his room, although he wanted nothing more than to do exactly that. Instead he went through the motions of presiding over the team dinner, coaches meeting and the other rituals that took up the night before a game. The next morning his first waking thought was that the evening before was a bad dream. But within seconds he remembered it had really happened.

Chapter Nine

The Lincoln State Abes continued their surprising resurgence with another close win, this one against the Tennessee Volunteers. As he watched the game end on TV, Jake thought that the football gods were smiling on Lincoln State this season like he had never seen them smile on any team before. The non-conference schedule that looked so daunting at the start of the season had turned out to be more winnable than anyone could have imagined. When the schedule was set, it appeared that the Abes were facing powerhouse, nationally ranked teams. But fortunately these teams were having rare mediocre seasons. Lincoln State's record now stood at three wins and just one loss, and that was a narrow defeat.

Like their previous wins, the Abes started fast against Tennessee and gained an early 10-0 lead, which shut down the noise from the usually raucous Volunteers fans. Led by Ono-lulo Kahona, the Lincoln State defense dominated the rest of the game, which ended with the Abes winning 17-11 in a game that wasn't as close as the score indicated.

Reporters at the press conference following the game no-ticed that coach Slim Haskins was unusually subdued. He answered questions politely and seemed happy about the outcome, but he didn't act like a coach whose team was on the brink of an incredible Cinderella season. As the reporters filed out of the press conference, a few commented quietly to each other that Slim Haskins must be under strict orders to avoid another meltdown like he had a few weeks before. That was the only possible explanation for his sudden change in behavior.

The funeral of Jennifer Stewart was held on the Monday fol-lowing her death. The coroner's report was released on Sun-day and officially listed the cause of death as homicide from the force of a blunt object to the head. The weapon appar-ently was a carved granite statue taken from Jennifer's fire-place mantle and left on the floor. Unfortunately, no finger prints were found anywhere in the apartment, including the statue.

Harvey asked Jake, Molly and Milt to accompany him to Jen-nifer's funeral in the Chicago suburbs. As usual, Sheila El-wood had social plans that kept her in Springfield on that day. Milt drove his Cadillac SUV with Harvey next to him in the front seat, and Molly and Jake shared the back seat.

The ride to the funeral was subdued. Jake noted that Harvey was particularly quiet.

About a half hour into the trip back to Springfield, Molly couldn't stand the silence anymore. "That was a great win on Saturday," Molly said enthusiastically, trying to break the gloom that hung thickly inside the passenger compartment.

Jake joined in, "It sure was. We're three-and-one going into the conference season."

"I think we can run the table and win the rest of our conference games," Milt chimed in as he drove, "but then we have that road game against Florida in November. That will be a tough one. But if we beat Florida, we could go to the big championship game!"

"I don't know about that," Molly countered, "remember how the bowl system works. The odds are pretty much stacked against a smaller school like Lincoln State."

"The good old Bowl Championship Series," Milt said, "How did college football ever get so screwed up?"

The Bowl Championship Series, commonly called the BCS, was created as a result of what many fans believed were unfair results in the national college football rankings. Instead of resolving the problem, the BCS ended up creating a complex system more geared toward maximizing profit than generating a true national champion, and was tilted very much in the favor of the major football conferences.

The desire for a national championship game always existed to some extent but momentum began to snowball in 1992, when the University of Miami Hurricanes and the University of Washington Huskies were considered the strongest teams in the nation. The major bowl games had standing agreements with the large conferences, making it almost impossible for the top two teams to meet one another in a bowl game. In 1992, the Washington Huskies were contractually locked into the Rose Bowl as the Pacific Ten champion to play against Big Ten champion Michigan, who was not highly ranked in the national standings. Because of their contractual obligation to the Rose Bowl, Washington could not play highly ranked Miami, who was committed to playing in the Orange Bowl. Both teams won their bowl games convincingly and ended up sharing the national championship.

Over the years, other teams won the national championship despite playing what many fans felt were weak schedules. One example was the Brigham Young University Cougars, who ended the 1984 season as the only undefeated team in the nation. However, they were a member of the poorly-regarded Western Athletic Conference and many felt that they played an inferior schedule.

To solve these and similar situations, the five most powerful conferences (and independent Notre Dame) contracted with six of the major bowl games to create the Bowl Coalition, which was created with the goal of resulting in a de facto "national championship game" between the top two teams in the nation.

Instead of settling anything, the Bowl Coalition was the start of two decades of squabbling by athletic directors and fans. Because other conferences were excluded, the Bowl Coalition made it impossible for a team from a non-Bowl Coalition conference to win a national championship. The system also did not include the Big Ten and Pacific Ten champions, which were both obligated to play in the Rose Bowl. In 1994, undefeated Penn State from the Big Ten played the Pacific Ten's University of Oregon in the Rose Bowl, while undefeated Nebraska played Miami in the Orange Bowl. If the system really paired the two top-ranked teams, Penn State would have played Nebraska for the national championship. That event was a fatal blow to the Bowl Coalition, which ended after only two years.

The Bowl Coalition was slightly restructured for the 1995 season and renamed the Bowl Alliance. Five conferences and three bowls participated. The championship game was intended to rotate among the three bowls. The Bowl Alliance had the same flaws as the Bowl Coalition: it still did not include the Pacific Ten or Big Ten champions, the Rose Bowl, or any non-Bowl Alliance teams.

Once again, a tweak in the bowl system and a name change was made. The Bowl Alliance was reformed into the Bowl Championship Series (usually called the BCS) for the 1998 season. The Rose Bowl agreed to release the Big Ten and Pacific Ten champions if they qualified for a national championship game. In return, the Rose Bowl was added to the yearly national championship rotation and the game was able to keep its desirable TV time slot in the late afternoon of New Year's Day.

Beginning with the 2006 season, the BCS National Championship Game became a separate, second bowl game played a week after New Year's Day at the same site as one of the four BCS member bowls. The new Bowl Championship Series not only added the Big Ten and the Pacific Ten conferences but also made an effort to include teams from smaller, mid-major conferences. Teams from the less powerful conferences could qualify for one of the BCS bowl games, supposedly including the National Championship game.

The plan sounded fair to all schools and all conferences on paper, but the fact is that no team outside of the six BCS-aligned conferences has ever played in the BCS Championship Game. The odds were incredibly stacked against schools like Lincoln State. For all practical purposes they had to finish undefeated while playing a challenging non-conference schedule and then win whatever conference they belonged to. And that only got them considered for the BCS Championship Game. They would still have to be ranked first or second in the nation based on a complicated ranking system.

Regarding the other four BCS Bowl games, the powerful member conferences had standing agreements to occupy almost all of the slots in the four BCS Bowl games, but the BCS allowed up to two non-member conference teams into a BCS bowl each year. Smaller schools had to "qualify" by being ranked among the top fourteen teams in the nation at the end of the regular season in order to even be considered for selection.

Boise State was the model that many small schools like Lincoln State tried to emulate. Playing in the mildly-regarded Western Athletic Conference, the Broncos were undefeated in 2006 and earned a spot in the 2007 Tostitos Fiesta Bowl against powerful Oklahoma. Sports experts predicted that Oklahoma would destroy Boise State and put to rest the notion that smaller schools had any place playing in a BCS Bowl. Instead, the Broncos won the game and validated the claim that small schools could compete against the "big boys."

The small-versus-large school controversy continued in spite of the four win-and-one loss record that the non-BCS conference teams racked up against teams from the qualifying conferences in the BCS Bowl games they have were allowed to play in during the first decade of the 2000s. The performances of Texas Christian and Boise State University fueled the argument for including the small schools in the BCS.

As they made the three-hour drive back to Springfield, Molly, Jake and Milt debated the chances of Lincoln State earning a BCS bowl slot while Harvey sat quietly.

"We obviously have to win out the rest of our games," Milt said, "or we don't stand a chance. But we could get into a BCS game with one loss."

"I don't want to be negative but I think one loss is already one too many," Molly countered, "It's virtually impossible to make it with anything but a perfect record. The deck is too stacked against us."

"I agree with Molly," Jake said, "according to the BCS rules, as an at-large team, Lincoln State would have to be ranked in the top fourteen teams to even be eligible. With one loss, it'll be a challenge to crack the top fourteen."

"And don't forget the ridiculous voting system," Molly added, "a Big Ten or Southeastern Conference team with one loss will always be ranked in the top fourteen before Lincoln State. The smaller conferences just don't get respect from the voters. It's a vicious circle: the system doesn't allow smaller schools to play the best teams in a BCS bowl, so the voters don't respect us, and because small schools don't get respect in the national polls we don't get a chance to play in the big bowl games."

"The BCS claims that computers determine the rankings," Milt said bitterly, "the computers do the math, but all of the voting is done by humans, and biased humans at that. All the computers do is tabulate faulty human voting."

Jake decided to put an end to the debate, "We can complain as much as we want, but remember that we still have to win the rest of our conference games and also beat Florida to even stand a chance. Let's see if we can do that and then we can complain that we got screwed."

On the ride back it became obvious to Jake and Molly that Harvey was taking Jennifer's death extremely hard. Molly tried to bring Harvey into the conversation on the return trip to Springfield, but he answered even direct questions with a few mumbled words. Harvey acted like he was a million miles away and not particularly happy to be there.

After another restless night, first thing Tuesday morning Harvey dug out the business card of Detective Eddie Martin and picked up his office phone. He dialed the extension listed on it.

"Detective Martin? This is Harvey Elwood calling."

"Mr. Elwood, what can I do for you?"

"I was just curious about something. As I mentioned to you, Jennifer Stewart was working on a special project for me. I gave her a small voice recorder and she was keeping verbal notes on. Did the recorder turn up anywhere? Did she have it with her, in her pocket? Or maybe it was found in her apartment?"

Eddie Martin picked up the file and grabbed the list of evidence and possessions to double check, even though he could almost recite the list from memory. "I don't see anything like that, Mr. Elwood."

Harvey frowned into the phone. The recorder wasn't there! "OK, detective. If it should turn up, could you please give it to me? It had details of a project and might it contain rather sensitive information."

"Will do, Mr. Elwood. But we carried out a very extensive search of the crime scene and if it wasn't found it's unlikely that she had it."

Harvey couldn't resist asking, "Are there any new developments in the case?"

"Not at this time. I may call you to get additional background on Ms. Stewart if that becomes necessary. You seem to have a high level of interest, for the victim being just your...assistant. You two must have worked very closely together."

Christ on a cross, what was that comment all about? Harvey mustered up his best easy going tone and answered, "No problem, I would be glad to help any way I can. I greatly appreciate your hard work on the case. Thanks again." Harvey hung up and put his face into his hands for thirty seconds. He picked up his phone and dialed Jake Goodman, "Jake, could I see you in my office? Come on up right now if you're not busy."

Jake sat down in a plush leather chair facing Harvey's desk. "What would you like to talk about, Harvey?"

"I have a favor to ask you, Jake. Sort of a sensitive issue, and I need to ask you to keep this just between us."

Jake was puzzled. "What is it?"

"Jennifer Stewart was my personal assistant, and I was quite fond of her. In fact, we were very close. As you probably know, Sheila and I have no children, and I sort of...well, I thought of Jennifer as my daughter."

The revelation from Harvey wasn't a complete surprise to Jake. Harvey seemed unusually despondent since Jennifer's death. And Ellen had told Jake about the gossip among female staffers that Harvey and Jennifer were "very close." Of course the gossip speculated on the most salacious of possibilities, not a father-daughter relationship like Harvey described it.

"I didn't know that. I'm sorry for your loss, Harvey."

"Thank you. Here is what I'd like you to do. I want to keep tabs on what's happening with the investigation of her death. But frankly, Jake, I'm just too damn close to the situation. It destroys my insides to have to talk about it. There is a detective by the name of Eduardo Martin who I've been in contact with; he's apparently in charge of the investigation. I'd like you to introduce yourself to him. Tell him you are representing the athletic department in keeping tabs on progress; that you have been receiving calls from the Chicago media asking what's going on down here."

Jake wasn't getting any calls from the Chicago media and Harvey knew it. The Chicago reporters had the phone number for the Springfield Police Department and they could get information anytime they wanted, straight from the source. Somewhere in the corner of Jake's brain a tiny alarm sounded – Harvey's request simply didn't add up.

Harvey continued, "Follow the progress of the case, and report to me if there are any new developments. And, please Jake, let's keep this under our hats. I've heard the rumors floating around the athletic office, and I don't want to give people any more to talk about."

What could Jake say? The way Harvey was asking him, there wasn't any way he could answer no. "Sure, I'll do it, Harvey. Do you have a phone number for this detective?"

As soon as Jake left his office, Harvey got up and told his assistant he had a meeting with the football coach. He walked down the steps and through the cavernous hallway under the stands of the stadium toward the football office. It was time to have a serious talk with Slim Haskins.

Chapter Ten

Jake counted fifteen reporters and camera men packed into the small media room at the Springfield Police headquarters; a few were standing but most of them were seated uncomfortably in blue plastic bucket chairs. The walls of the room were battleship-gray painted cinderblock and the government-standard linoleum was years past its prime. Three cameras from Springfield television stations were aimed at the podium in the front of the room. Detective Eddie Martin walked in briskly, stepped behind the podium and nodded to the audience.

"Good afternoon, everyone. In case we haven't met, I'm Detective Eduardo Martin, the lead detective on the Jennifer Stewart case. We received the Coroner's report," Martin began, "and the report determined the cause of death to be homicide as a result of blunt trauma to the head."

A half-dozen hands shot toward the ceiling before Eddie finished the sentence.

"Detective Martin!" yelled a television reporter, "Are there any suspects? Any arrest made?"

"No arrests made and I'm not in a position to discuss suspects at this time," Eddie sidestepped. He didn't want to discuss the fact that there was no suspect. There wasn't even anything close to a suspect.

"How about evidence? Murder weapon? Fingerprints?" asked another reporter.

Eddie answered, "We believe the murder weapon was a decorative stone statue that we found near the body. Photos we found indicate that it was the property of the victim, and was probably removed from the fireplace mantle. Other than that we can't discuss evidence at this point in the investigation."

The detective suppressed a grimace and put on his best poker face. He knew for a fact there were a lot of prints in the apartment, every one of them smudged and unusable. Whoever the killer was, they took their time and cleaned up pretty well. Forensics picked up some dirt samples from the carpet, but those could have come from anyone. The victim was a graduate student and according to friends, she was not in line to receive any awards for her housekeeping skills. So the carpet soil samples could have been one day old, or one year old. The most promising evidence was possible DNA found on Jennifer Stewart's bashed-in head, but that would take several weeks to analyze.

After a few more questions, the reporters surmised that there was no more newsworthy information forthcoming, and the press conference ended. Jake lingered to catch Eddie and introduce himself.

"Detective Martin, I'm Jake Goodman, the Sports Information Director with Lincoln State."

Eddie Martin shook Jake's hand. "Good to meet you, Jake. Isn't the Sports Information Director's job to hold press conferences, not to *attend* press conferences?"

"Under normal circumstances, I wouldn't be here. But this is a new situation for the athletic department; we've never had anything like this happen. I want to make sure that I have the latest information so if I'm asked I know what I'm talking about. I would appreciate it if you would keep me in the loop on new developments in the case."

"Sure," Eddie said, "why not. I'll make sure you're kept informed of major stuff, along with the press."

Just then, Jake saw Johnny Rose approach them. To Jake's surprise, Johnny slapped Eddie Martin on the back good naturedly. "That was a riveting performance, Eddie. I almost stayed awake through all of it which is more than I can say for most of your press conferences."

"Jesus Christ, Johnny. What are you doing here? I thought you'd be covering the Bingo tournament at the old folk's home this afternoon."

"I got promoted," Johnny said, "I cover Jake's turf now. This whole unfortunate mess being related to Lincoln State sports, I thought I better see what's happening. I figured you'd announce you already cracked the case."

"This is off the record, OK guys? Do you know what we've got on this case? Precisely dick. And the pressure is already on. This is the highest profile case I've ever been involved with. My typical murder case is figuring out which junkie killed another junkie, and they usually leave an evidence trail that's so easy to follow, Helen Keller could track them down. Also, usually no one gives a shit if we arrest the right junkie or not. The powers-that-be figure a junkie must be guilty of *something*, so if we arrest the wrong junkie it's no big deal; they all belong in prison anyway."

"I'm a brother, man. You don't need to tell me about Springfield PD's enlightened approach to criminal justice," Johnny said, "But on the Jennifer Stewart case, there isn't anything at all to go on?"

"Listen, it's only been six days. Usually in a case like this, it's forensics that will give us early leads. I'm not sure if we're dealing with a professional job here or it was just an amateur killer that got lucky. But the crime scene was very clean, the cleanest I've seen in a long time. There is one thing...it isn't evidence, which is why I didn't feel obligated to bring it up at the press conference. Plus, we haven't told the victim's family yet; we'll do that later today and release it to the press then. The dead girl was pregnant."

"Huh," Johnny said, "How far along was she?"

"Not that far. About eight weeks. She just found out herself not that long ago, judging from the medical test reports that we found in her apartment."

"Any idea who the papa was?" Johnny asked.

"No, but we're working on it." All three men stood silent for several moments trying to absorb the news.

Jake finally broke the silence and said, "You know, it occurs to me we all have access to information on this. If we all stay alert, maybe we can share what we find and help each other out."

Eddie Martin was skeptical, "What are you going to uncover that will help me, Mr. Newly-hired Sports Information Director? Sounds like a one-way street."

"Jennifer worked in the athletic office and had quite a few girlfriends there," Jake said, "It seems to me that they know quite a bit about her life. One of her friends may have been close enough to be a confidant. And they'll be much more likely to tell me sensitive stuff, more likely than telling a police detective."

Johnny piped in, "Even a suave, debonair poe-leez-man like you can't get all the answers if he's coming in from the outside. Jake has a point, Eddie. You'd have to spend days interviewing employees and chasing dead ends to find out what Jake can find out in a couple of conversations with the right people. And what contacts Jake doesn't have at Lincoln State, I have. The three of us can work together and all come out ahead. You solve the case, Jake keeps up on the happs, and I get an exclusive story when you make an arrest."

"I don't know about you getting an exclusive," Eddie laughed, "I suppose I can give you a few hours head start when we break the case."

"It's a deal then," Johnny said. They all shook hands, then Jake and Johnny walked out of the police building together.

"You're full of surprises," Jake said, "how do you guys know each other?"

"You lost touch with my career for a while there, bro, while you were over in Iraq playing in the sand. My first job with the paper was junior reporter on the courthouse beat. I did that for a few years before I got moved over to sports. Eddie and I go way back; he's a good guy."

"Will he do what he said and let us know what's going on?"

"Yeah, but I suggest that you start schmoozing the gals in the athletic department, especially the ones who were close to Jennifer Stewart. Throw Eddie the first bone and let him know that you're willing to do your part. Maybe you can even figure out who the baby daddy was."

"I'll get to work, Johnny. Stay in touch." Jake got in his car and started the ignition.

***

Harvey decided to talk with Slim Haskins in a private place where they would not be overheard. What was more private than the vacant stands of the football stadium on a Tuesday afternoon? He dialed the coach's extension and told him to meet him in the bleachers on the east side of the stadium.

Slim Haskins sat down near Harvey but left a few feet between them. There was no one else in sight. "I never get to see this view," he said as he gazed out on the empty field.

"Me either," Harvey said and then paused. No sense worrying about niceties. "You did it, didn't you Haskins? You killed her."

The response was quick and pleading, "I did not! Don't throw around accusations you can't back up."

It was time for a bluff. Harvey said with false certainty, "I know you were there that night. Jennifer texted me that you were at her door."

Slim's face turned pale. "OK, I was there. I'm not denying it. But she was alive when I left! I'm telling the truth!"

"I need to know this. Did you take anything – anything at all – from her apartment? Take anything from her pockets?"

Harvey noted that Slim looked genuinely confused by the question. He answered, "No, I didn't take anything. Why would I take anything? All we did was talk for a couple of minutes. It wasn't a friendly conversation. We argued, but I didn't kill her."

"I have to go to the police, Haskins. I don't have a choice in this," Harvey said.

Haskins' face contorted with fear and anger, "Are you forgetting what I know? And about the pictures I still have? You call the cops and I'll tell them everything I know about you lovebirds. Show them a little slideshow of the two of you knocking boots. Then they'll have a pair of suspects to choose from – me and you. Where were you that night, Harvey?"

Harvey thought for several seconds. He was at home that night – alone. Sheila had gone out and he thought about calling Jennifer but needed to catch up on some paperwork. He remembered dozing off while watching Thursday night football on television. Sheila got home about 10 p.m. which left Harvey with two or three hours unaccounted for and absolutely no alibi.

Harvey said, "I won't say anything – for now. But I don't buy your story. You were there and Jennifer died that night. If I was on the jury I'd vote for you to go to prison, you fucking lowlife asshole."

Slim stood up, "Harvey - one more thing. You'd better start working on my contract renewal." Haskins turned and walked away.

Harvey walked back to his office and slammed the door. He was seething. Haskins knew he had him by the balls. When push came to shove, there was no evidence Haskins was at Jennifer's apartment that night. It would be Slim's word against Harvey's. If the police found out about their affair – and that Jennifer's baby was his – they would peg Harvey as a much better suspect than a football coach who Jennifer barely had any contact with.

With a home game against Eastern Carolina coming up Saturday, everyone involved was focused on their jobs. Harvey stayed on top of Milt, who attended to the many details of making sure the game would go smoothly. There were vendors, security, ticket takers and ushers to take care of; Milt had to make sure everyone was scheduled and would show up on Saturday. The athletic department used outside services for everything but the vendors. For the food and drink counters, volunteers from non-profit groups provided the manpower, in exchange for a percentage of the profits. Middle school-aged kids were hired to walk the stands. Most of the planning was done long before the season started but there were a lot of loose ends to keep track of during game week.

Jake spent the early part of the week sending stories to the newspapers, radio and television stations as well as coordinating media interviews with football players and coaches. The Abes were starting to attract a small amount of national attention because of their record, and Jake fielded a few calls from ESPN and other national media.

Later in the week, Jake once again was faced with the need for major damage-control. His phone rang just before 1:00 a.m. Friday morning. It was Johnny Rose.

"Hey, Sleeping Beauty. You better wake up. Two of your football players are in the slammer, arrested tonight."

Jake was instantly awake and his mind raced. "Three questions, Johnny. Who are they, what are they accused of, and how in the hell do you find these things out so fast?"

"I'll answer the last question first, my friend. I know the right people. They help me out. Who were the players? Two benchwarmers – sophomores, and their only playing time is during the last minute or two in blow out games, if that. They're charged with battery; the word is they beat the crap out of some freshman punks who were giving them a hard time. The two punks are in the hospital."

"What time did this happen?"

"Not that long ago, around midnight. Doesn't your football coach enforce a curfew?"

"I would think so, but since there is no athletic dormitory, I assume these guys were living in an apartment or student dorm with no one watching over them every minute. We did a little sneaking around after curfew in our time, didn't we?"

"Yeah, but we didn't get snot-slinging drunk and beat people up. There's a difference between being a rambunctious college kid and a criminal."

"Thanks for the tip," Jake said, "Are you going to put this in today's paper?"

"Too late for the morning edition," Johnny said, "it'll be in the afternoon paper, probably front page of sports under the fold. But don't roll over in bed and go back to sleep. Remember that the television news will be all over this first thing tomorrow. Your bad luck – last year no one gave a shit about the Abes, but this season they're winning so people are paying attention. This is going to be a news story, Jake, whether you like it or not."

"OK, I'm on it. Thanks again. I gotta go." Jake hung up the phone and slid out of bed.

Chapter Eleven

Jake's first thought was to call Harvey Elwood. A sleepy Sheila answered and after a minute or two of rustling and muffled conversation, Harvey got on the phone.

"Harvey, sorry to bother you at this hour but I just learned that two football players were arrested tonight. They're accused of beating up two students outside a bar downtown."

"Shit. There's not much I can do about it tonight but I'll be ready for the questions tomorrow morning. I'll call Milt, it's his job to get the legal stuff untangled. I assume you know all the particulars as far as talking to the press."

"Not yet, but I'm heading down to the jail right now. I'll know everything I need to know in an hour or two."

"All right. You know, it's Slim Haskins and his crappy recruiting policies that get us into bullshit situations like this." With those words, Harvey hung up.

Jake held a press conference at 7 a.m. Friday to provide reporters with the details. Although the press conference was attended by every major media outlet in the Springfield area, players being arrested for a fight was not enough to cause much of a stir. After a couple of questions, the reporters were more interested in talking about Saturday's game than about the arrested players. The players were already out of jail, having been bailed out by Milt in the wee hours of the morning.

Johnny was at the press conference, looking particularly disheveled from having slept little the night before. He approached Jake as the other reporters left the media room.

"You look like hell," Jake told Johnny.

"I feel like it too. I've got to stop jumping out of bed every time a Lincoln State player gets arrested. I'm losing too much sleep."

Jake didn't take the bait. He said, "Since you haven't been sleeping anyway, have you found out anything on the Jennifer Stewart case?"

"No chance yet, but I assume you haven't been able to talk to anyone either. We've both been up to our eyeballs in work the past couple of days."

"I have a date with Ellen on Saturday night. I know she wasn't particularly close to Jennifer but I'm betting that she'll know who was."

"You got off easy today, Jake. The Springfield press corps is too excited about the possibility of a bowl game to get too bent out of shape about a couple of arrests for fighting."

"I know, but sooner or later Haskins' recruiting strategy will get Lincoln State into big trouble. You know what he says about small schools only being able to 'recruit kids with either character or talent but not both.'"

"He has a valid argument, at least sort of. Smaller Division I colleges usually end up with the recruits that the major schools turn down for one reason or another. Some kids don't have the talent to make it in a big school but can contribute at a smaller school. Others have plenty of talent but also have criminal records."

"I know," Jake answered, "If a kid with legal problems has superstar talent, the big schools will usually take him anyway. If he's very good but not a superstar, the kid often gets ignored by the big schools and ends up at a program like Lincoln State."

Many Division I colleges have been known to ignore the off-field background of recruits. A 2011 study by *Sports Illustrated* and CBS News found that one in every fourteen student athletes got in trouble with the law, either before they were recruited or during their college years. Nearly 40% of the incidents found in the study were serious offenses, including assault and battery, domestic violence, aggravated assault, robbery and sex offenses. There were also charges uncovered for drug and alcohol offenses, including DUI and intent to distribute cocaine.

Another study, by Benedict and Crosset, found that one-third of all sexual assaults on the thirty campuses the study examined were committed by male student athletes, even though this group made up only three percent of the overall student body. Still other research done at Georgetown University found that the crime rate among varsity athletes was double the arrest rate of the general student population.

Johnny said, "You know what would be a great start? If Lincoln State performed background checks on potential recruits. Very few colleges bother to even do that. If colleges don't look at the kid's background, they won't find anything that would keep them from recruiting him."

"Good idea. But many states don't allow access to the criminal records of minors. But we could still have potential recruits informally checked out. Everybody knows when a kid has been in trouble with the law, it's no secret. But college recruiters would rather play dumb – you know what they say, ignorance is bliss."

Jake continued, "I don't buy into the argument Slim Haskins makes. Some successful college programs have succeeded in avoiding recruitment of student-criminals. How about Texas Christian University? They're a small conference school that has had great football teams and I read recently they have had very few problems with players being arrested."

"Yeah, I read that story too," Johnny said, "They won the Rose Bowl in 2011 and did not have one single player in trouble with the law that season."

Jake added, "And you can look at our basketball program

here at Lincoln State. We win games, but the arrest rate among basketball players over the past five years is lower than the student body as a whole. It boils down to a coach doing the hard work to find players who have both the character and the talent to make it at a school like Lincoln State. It can be done. I like what Steve Jefferies tells his assistants about evaluating the character of basketball recruits. He says, 'If you wouldn't hire that athlete to babysit your kids then we don't want him at Lincoln State.'"

"Well, let's keep our fingers crossed that no more problems come up because that can be a distraction away from making a major bowl," Johnny said, "It would be exciting to see the Abes in a big bowl game. Plus I could use a nice trip to Florida or California in January."

"I'll keep my fingers crossed for both of us," Jake said, "See you on Saturday in the press box."

Although the local press didn't make a big deal out of the arrests, Elliot Trentwood, one of the Athletic Board members, took it upon himself to tell his opinion to any reporter who would listen. "Lincoln State needs to take a stand against criminal athletes," he said, "and the football program has been the biggest offender by far. Over three-quarters of all athletes arrested at this school are from the football team and that reflects on the head coach and staff. At the next board meeting, I intend to make a motion that Donald Haskins' contract not be renewed following this season."

Harvey Elwood had considerable authority in the operation of the athletic department, but the ultimate power was held by the Athletic Board, the members of whom were appointed by the Lincoln State Board of Trustees. This was especially true of decisions about contract renewals for coaches and key department personnel. Five of the seven members respected Harvey's opinion and his ability to run the department, Elliot Trentwood was one of two board members who enjoyed meddling as much as they possibly could.

***

Slim Haskins sat alone in his office late Friday night. He was supposed to be making final preparations for the game but instead, his mind was racing. He had the leverage he needed with Harvey, no question about it. But having heard that stuffed-shirt idiot Trentwood spouting off to the press, Slim doubted for the first time that having Harvey under his thumb would be enough to get his contract renewed. It was ironic, Slim thought, that he had survived so many seasons with mediocre win-loss records and now his team was doing great and he might find himself kicked to the curb.

He was also worried about the conversation he had with Harvey Elwood. Harvey was convinced that Slim took something from Jennifer Stewart's apartment – what could that have been? Was there something incriminating in the apartment sitting there like a ticking time bomb waiting to be found by the police? If the police did find something why hadn't he been questioned yet? He forced himself to stop thinking about it. The best way to avoid all of this shit was to win the rest of this season's games. He remembered a head coach he worked for telling him that winning was like an invincibility shield. The coach had told him, "As long as you're winning championships it would take being con-victed of murder to get a head coach fired." Slim smiled rue-fully at the wall in his empty office...a poor choice of words, he thought.

Saturday's game against Eastern Carolina turned out to be a great win for Lincoln State. The Abes won easily in a 40-3 blowout and dominated the game from beginning to end. The offense played flawlessly and Eastern Carolina was over-whelmed by the Lincoln State defense.

In spite of all the problems swirling around Slim Haskins, he was jubilant in the post-game interviews. "Lincoln State is the real deal," the coach proclaimed, "no one can deny that after this performance."

"How do you feel about our bowl game chances?" a reporter asked Haskins.

"Hold on there, son," Haskins answered, arms outstretched with his palms held out, "It's way too early to mention that sort of thing. We are four-and-one. We still have five confer-ence games to play, three of them on the road. And we also have a really tough road game against Florida. We're taking things one game at a time. We don't want to be looking too far ahead and end up blowing a game."

Later in the press conference, a young reporter from the local sports radio station was emboldened by Slim's buoyant mood and decided to ask the question all the other reporters were afraid to ask, "Coach, do you have any comment on El-liot Trentwood's statement he made this week?"

The room fell silent for a long moment before Slim Haskins let loose with a hearty, loud laugh and said, "I think he's full of hot air. Do you think the board will vote in the middle of the season not to renew the contract for a coach who is having the best year in school history?"

A few nervous giggles floated around the room. Obviously, most of the reporters expected a classic Slim Haskins meltdown and were relieved to hear his casual response.

Jake did his usual after-game duties, marshaling players to and from the interview room and occasionally interjecting additional information when it was appropriate. Harvey stopped Jake and remarked after the interviews were over, "Jake, you seem like a real natural for this job. That whole post-game was handled perfectly and you did a fantastic job earlier this week dealing with the press. You've only been at it a few months and you act like a seasoned professional."

"Thanks, Harvey. I appreciate that."

"You deserve the praise, Jake. Say...on that other project I assigned you, is there any news to report?"

"The police don't have much to go on. One thing I learned, and you probably heard on the news, is that Jennifer Stewart was pregnant."

"I heard that. It is very unfortunate and sad. So the police have no leads at all?"

"Nothing," Jake answered. He thought for an instant about mentioning the agreement he made with Eddie and Johnny but for some reason thought he should keep it to himself. He decided to change the subject, "What did you think of the coach's answer to the question about the athletic board?"

"As much as I hate to admit it, I think Haskins is right. The board would be foolish to make a decision in the middle of the season. And we need to look at data from other schools on their arrests of athletes. Remember, the football team has a hundred players so it isn't unexpected that they have the highest number of arrests."

It turned out that Harvey's prediction was completely right. At the Tuesday board meeting, Elliot Trentwood's motion was not seconded by any other board members and was dismissed without any discussion.

Saturday night, Jake and Ellen had a quiet dinner off campus, although it was difficult to avoid Lincoln State fans, raucously celebrating the big home win. Ellen's job in the athletic department was assistant ticket manager and game days were just as busy for her as they were for Jake.

"You should have seen what happened today," Ellen said, "Like every game, there were a few ticket misprints that end up with people fighting over the same seat. Last year that was no problem, we would just park one of them in an unsold, empty seat. There were plenty of empty seats last year. We always have maybe a dozen tickets for empty seats on hand to resolve problems that come up. Guess what? That dumb ass Milt set up the extra tickets and all of them were printed for the same exact seat!"

"Uh oh," Jake said, "that sounds like trouble."

"It sure was," Ellen said laughing, "Instead of a dozen fans being a little pissed off to be moved to other seats, we had a dozen people screaming and fighting over one seat."

"Jeez, what happened?"

"One guy got a bloody nose, among other things. He and another guy with the same ticket were going at it pretty good. Fortunately, the stadium security didn't overreact and arrest anyone. We were able to squeeze the fans into the administration's luxury box. Those people went from being extremely angry to thinking they had hit the lottery. They got the best seats in the house and free food to boot. One lady had a hot dog in each hand every time I looked at her. She must have downed a dozen of them."

***

Jake and Ellen's date ended with Jake spending the night at Ellen's apartment. As they lay still in bed, both spent from lovemaking, Jake steered the talk toward Jennifer Stewart.

"I met the detective in charge of the investigation this week," Jake said, "he told me he wasn't able to find out much about Jennifer Stewart's personal life. I suspect he isn't talking to the right people on campus. Did she have any good friends in the department?"

"Yes she did. She really was pretty mature for a graduate assistant and didn't really hang out with other students that much. She preferred to hang out with people she worked with in the athletic office. I believe her best friends were a couple of women who work on the second floor. I always saw them going to lunch together and talking in the break room."

"I have a favor to ask, a big one. Can you set me up to talk to them, informally? I'd like to find out more about their relationship. I have this feeling that they haven't told the police everything they know."

"Since when did you become a crime investigator? Don't you have enough to do?" Ellen asked.

"I'm just curious, that's all. I have this feeling in my gut that this whole thing involves someone in the athletic office. And that worries me."

"All right, Sherlock," Ellen said, "how about I see if I can get the two of them to go to lunch with me? Then you can run into us, accidently on purpose."

"Sounds like a plan," Jake said, and slid closer to Ellen, "how about another favor as long as you're being so agreeable?"

Chapter Twelve

Jake's Monday started with his weekly meeting with Molly Bennett to review publicity for the women's side of the athletic program. The success of the football team was definitely helping the Lincoln State women's sports. Enthusiasm about the Abes in the local community was at an all-time high and rubbed off a little on all of the other sports.

Soccer was the biggest fall sport for women and attendance was well ahead of the previous year. Throughout the season, Jake and Molly provided a steady stream of human-interest stories about the women soccer players to the media, carefully timed to coincide with home games. The season was winding down and Jake laid out his plans for the final weeks of the schedule. When they were done, the conversation turned to other topics.

"Jake," Molly said, "do you know the best thing you could do to give a boost to Lincoln State women's sports? Get the school to change the team name. For Christ's sake, we call our women's teams the 'Lady Abes,' which has to be the stupidest name in the history of college sports."

"I don't want to rub it in," Jake teased, "but didn't the Lady Abes make the ten worst college sports nicknames in *USA Today* a few years ago?"

"Of course it did, how could it not be one of the worst names ever? Our women's teams go to other schools and they are ridiculed. They call us the 'Mary Todds,' which was the name of Lincoln's wife. And she was best known for being certifiably insane. Opposing teams' fans come to our games with Lincoln beards on to mock us!"

"Lincoln State's nickname has been around for a hundred years," Jake reminded her, "there's nothing offensive about it, unless you're a woman athlete that has to wear it on her jersey. I don't think I can get anyone to go along with a change."

"Speaking of offensive, I bumped into that asshole Slim Haskins this morning. He struts around like he runs the whole athletic program," Molly complained.

"He acts as if he's immune to all the other problems he's had," Jake said, "but he should remember the other coaches who got fired in spite of winning records."

"Yeah, there was Tressel at Ohio State University not that long ago. He ran a football program that looked squeaky-clean, but when he found out that there were problems with some of his players violating NCAA rules, he ignored it and covered it up instead of reporting the violations to the administration," Molly said.

"He's just one example. You can go back through the years, coaches like Barry Switzer at Oklahoma, Pat Dye at Auburn, Nueheisel at Washington and lots of other coaches all either got canned or quit under pressure, even though they were successful on the field."

"I'd be willing to bet that Slim Haskins has a lot of stuff he knows about but keeps under his hat."

"The problem is, when a school is having a great year like we are, it attracts more scrutiny from everyone – the press and other schools start turning over rocks to see if they can find violations. If there's something to be found, this is when it's likely to come out."

"I'm surprised that Harvey hasn't been riding Haskins a lot harder about making sure everyone involved with football is keeping on the straight-and-narrow," Molly said.

Jake agreed, "Harvey really seems to be staying away from him. I don't know that I've even seen the two of them within a hundred feet of each other in the past month or so."

"They were never that tight to begin with," Molly said, "I think Harvey has been hoping to get rid of Haskins for the past couple of years."

"Well, if the season keeps up the way it's going, the board is almost certain to extend his contract."

"Unless something serious happens off the field...having winning teams didn't save those other coaches we just talked about, and one great season sure won't save Slim Haskins if all hell breaks loose. I gotta get going, Jake. Good to talk with you, as usual," Molly said as she left Jake's office.

Just as Molly walked out, Jake's phone rang. Ellen had set up a lunch with her two co-workers for the following day. The plan was for Jake to "accidentally" stumble into the trio as they had lunch. He would turn the discussion toward Jennifer Stewart and hopefully learn something.

Jake walked into The Feed Store, a bustling home cooking place on Adams Street, at twelve-fifteen and, sure enough, there was Ellen sitting with two women he had seen around the athletic offices. He tried to feign the appropriate look of surprise.

"Ellen! I didn't know you were having lunch out. I was downtown and just stopped by to grab a bowl of soup. They have amazing beef barley."

"Hi, Jake," Ellen said, "we just sat down a few minutes ago. This is Olivia and Anjali, we work together."

Jake could tell that Ellen was enjoying her acting role and could sense he was nervous. She gave him an almost-imperceptible, sly smile and said to her lunch mates, "Is it OK if Jake joins us?"

Olivia and Anjali were both in their mid-twenties. They had

observed Jake around the office and he was considered the most eligible bachelor in the athletic department. The prospect of having Jake join them for lunch was eagerly welcomed.

After they ordered and engaged in some chit-chat, Jake decided it was time to steer the conversation toward his objectives. "I heard that you two were good friends with Jennifer Stewart. I'm sorry about what happened to her."

"Yes, we were very close," Anjali said, "it was a terrible shock."

Right on cue, Ellen said, "I heard rumors around the department that she was seeing an older man."

Jake stayed with the script and answered, "Really? I hadn't heard that."

Olivia piped in, "We were close. Jennifer told us she was seeing someone, but never really came out and said who. Even though she tried to hide it, Anjali and I knew who it was."

Jake knew he had to proceed very carefully, but he sensed that Olivia was dying to tell someone this bit of news. He decided to try some reverse psychology. "I like office gossip as much as the next gal," he joked, "but I'm not sure this is something I want to know. In my position I am trusted with a lot of sensitive information so I know the importance of keeping a secret."

Olivia looked disappointed. Ellen quickly jumped in, "*I want to know*, Jake! Don't be such a poop! Honestly, Olivia, it will just be between us. We won't say a word to anyone in the department."

"It was pretty obvious that Jennifer had something going with Harvey Elwood," Olivia whispered, "The way her eyes sparkled when she talked about him and looked at him, she wasn't fooling us. We thought it was kind of disgusting. A fifty-year old married man?" Anjali made an appropriately repulsed face to express her agreement with Olivia.

Now that the floodgates had opened Jake became bolder and asked, "Do you think Harvey was the father of her baby? Did she mention to you whether or not she broke the news to the father?"

"He knew about the baby and it was his, all right," Anjali said, "Jennifer told him less than a week before she was killed. She said that he was shocked but not too upset. He told her that he preferred she get an abortion, but that he was supportive of whatever decision she made."

Olivia added, "She was leaning very strongly toward having the baby. We were trying to talk her out of it. I mean...there was no future between her and Harvey. But sometimes it seemed like she hoped there was."

"Right, like he would leave his wife, create a scandal and ruin his career! She was out of her mind if she thought there was any chance of that happening," Anjali said.

"The police talked to you both," Jake said, "they talked to everyone in the department. Did you tell them about Jennifer and Harvey?"

"No way," Olivia said, "we don't want this to blow up in our faces. I don't want reporters hounding me day and night."

"Me either," Anjali added, "Besides, Olivia and I talked about it and decided that Harvey couldn't have had anything to do with Jennifer's death. From everything she said, he was madly in love with her, and she wasn't the least bit afraid of him. All we would accomplish by telling the police is cause a big scandal for the athletic department. Harvey would probably get fired and that isn't what Jennifer would have wanted."

"The truth is we really don't know for one-hundred percent sure it was Harvey she was seeing, since Jennifer never came out and told us," Olivia said. The way she said it struck Jake as an excuse for knowingly withholding information from the police. It was obvious they knew it was Harvey.

Jake probed further, "Was this affair – was it something everyone knew about? I'm new in the office and not really in the loop. Was I just missing something that everyone else knew?"

"Jennifer kept it very much a secret," Olivia said, "She confided in us but we were the only ones who knew for sure she was even seeing someone. There was a lot of gossip around the office that she was seeing an older man but I think we were the only ones who figured out it was Harvey."

"Did Harvey's wife know?" Jake asked.

"Jennifer was pretty tense and stressed out the last couple of weeks," Anjali said, "We figured it was because of being pregnant. About a week before she died, she mentioned that she was worried the guy's wife was starting to suspect he was having an affair."

At that moment, the waitress delivered their food. Olivia and Anjali used the interruption to change the subject and Jake decided it would be too pushy to try for more information.

Driving back to the athletic offices, Jake's mind worked furiously. He was shocked at the revelation that Jennifer and Harvey were having an affair but he agreed with the assessment that Harvey could not possibly have been involved in Jennifer's murder. He recalled how devastated Harvey was after Jennifer's death – it should have been crystal clear that they were emotionally involved. Jake chastised himself for not putting the facts together sooner.

As long as he was out of the office anyway, Jake grabbed his cell phone and dialed Johnny Rose. "Hey buddy, it's Jake. I have news for you and Eddie."

Johnny said, "I was meeting Eddie for a beer in a couple of hours at D'Arcy's Pint. See you there. You're buying."

Jake walked into the Irish pub called D'Arcy's Pint. The pub opened in the late 1990s, but the owners used a lot of recycled wood and fixtures gave the place a feel like it had been there for decades. It was crowded, even on a Tuesday evening. Jake spotted Johnny and Eddie occupying a corner table and slid into the seat next to Johnny.

"I'll have a black and tan," Jake told the server.

"So what's this big news you have for me?" Eddie asked.

"What I'm going to tell you guys absolutely has to be off the record in terms of the press finding out," Jake said, "it would be devastating to the athletic program if this got out. Do I have your word on that?"

Eddie and Johnny traded glances for a few moments, and then agreed.

"Jennifer was having an affair with Harvey Elwood. He was the father of the baby."

"Fuck a duck!" Johnny said, "That is big news – but don't worry about me keeping it under my hat, Jake. That sort of thing falls under the category of hearsay and I don't write stories like that."

Jake turned toward Eddie to see his reaction, but Eddie was quiet. Jake could tell he was processing how this news affected his investigation.

"That definitely makes Harvey Elwood a person of interest," Eddie finally said, "but nothing more than that for now. I'll get together with him; make it seem like routine follow up questioning. But I have to tell you Jake, if he doesn't come clean and admit there was more than just a manager-employee relationship, I'm going to have to grill him pretty hard."

"Do what you need to do, Eddie. As long as we can keep this out of the news," Jake said, "that's all I want. But my feeling is that Harvey didn't kill her. I spent a lot of time with him in the days after Jennifer was killed and he was truly broken up."

"Now that you mention it," Eddie said, "Harvey showed up at Ms. Stewart's apartment building shortly after we found the body. As a cop, I could assume that he's the killer returning to the scene of the crime. If I was Sam Spade in a bad 1940s movie then I would buy that. But I talked to Elwood that day, and I think he was checking up on his girlfriend because he was worried about her. I could see it in his eyes when he found out she was dead – he was broken up but trying to hide his emotions."

"This is fascinating gossip," Johnny said, "but it really doesn't help with the case."

Eddie interrupted, "I don't think it implicates Harvey Elwood, but I'm willing to bet that somehow there's a link between the affair and the murder. This wasn't a random killing. There was no robbery, no sexual assault and no forced entry, which tells me that Jennifer Stewart knew the killer. She wasn't dating any classmates anyone knew of; her social life pretty much centered on people in the athletic department. I've got to assume that somehow, Harvey Elwood is linked to Jennifer Stewart's murder. Maybe not directly, but there is a connection."

"You're a regular Hispanic Sherlock Holmes," Johnny teased.

"What does that make you, the black Dr. Watson?" Eddie answered.

The three of them laughed, ordered another round of beers and talked football the rest of the night.

Chapter Thirteen

The morning after his dinner with Jake and Johnny, Eddie Martin called Harvey Elwood to request a follow-up interview. Eddie also asked for a follow-up interview with Jake, an idea that was suggested by Jake because he thought it would avoid suspicion that he was aiding the police investigation.

Harvey asked Eddie, "Is Jake Goodman or myself a suspect in the murder?"

"No, of course not," Eddie answered, "These are just routine follow-up interviews. I know much more about Ms. Stewart's personal life than I did a couple of weeks ago. I have some additional questions, that's all."

"Where do you want to do this?"

"I think it would be best if both you and Jake came down to my office."

Harvey hesitantly agreed and they settled on meeting early that afternoon.

Eddie had given a lot of thought about how to go at Harvey Elwood, and decided that the best strategy was to keep things friendly to try to catch Harvey off guard. If that didn't work, Eddie would crank up the pressure.

Jake's extension rang late Monday morning with the expected call from Harvey.

"Jake, you and I have been summoned to police headquarters to answer some additional questions about Jennifer Stewart's death," Harvey said, "I set up the meeting for two o'clock. Why don't we drive over together?"

Police headquarters was a short drive, but Harvey was determined to pump Jake for as much information as possible.

"So, Jake...if you don't mind me asking, why do you think you're being brought in for questioning?"

Jake had anticipated this question and had already settled on a plan to play dumb, "I haven't a clue. I didn't know Jennifer very well. I guess we'll find out shortly what detective Martin has in mind."

When they arrived, Eddie Martin greeted them and asked to speak with Jake first. His plan was to make Harvey sweat for a while in the dingy, dirty waiting area; Eddie figured that having Harvey rub elbows with the finest scumbags in Springfield for a half-hour would soften him up a bit.

Once the interview door closed, Eddie dropped his stern, formal countenance and smiled broadly at Jake.

"Did you see the look on Elwood's face? He looks as nervous as a virgin at a prison rodeo!"

"He's scared, that's for sure," Jake answered, "You're the detective and you probably have lots better instincts than me about stuff like this, but I'm still convinced that Harvey didn't kill her."

"I'd like to agree with you, Jake. But he's not being forthright. For one thing, I think he's lying about not being at Jennifer Stewart's on the night of the murder." Eddie pulled an eight-by-ten black and white glossy from an envelope and slid it across the table. It appeared to be a security camera photo of the street in front of Jennifer Stewart's apartment building.

"What's this?" Jake asked.

"See that Mercedes, Illinois license plate LSABES2? Guess who that vehicle is registered to? None other than Mr. Harvey Elwood. That photo was from camera footage taken the night of the murder."

"If there were security cameras all over the place doesn't that make your job a lot easier? You can see everyone who went into the building."

"I wish," Eddie said, "but the cameras were all screwed up

that night. The building has an old security system, one of those deals with VHS tapes that get re-used over and over again. They apparently cycle the tapes over a month – so the tape that got used on August first gets used again on September first and so on. We grabbed the tapes within a couple days of the murder, so we should have the night of the murder plus almost the entire previous month on tape. The problem is, the camera system is so screwed up that there are a lot of spots on the tapes where there's nothing but static. We know that Elwood's car was there for a while – I wish I knew for how long but there's no way to tell with all the static gaps and the fact their piece of crap system doesn't do a proper time stamp on the video. Unfortunately, there's no undamaged tape showing who came or went through the door to the building or when they were there. So I'm going to bluff and see if I can get Elwood to spill everything he knows."

"Is there a resident manager or anybody like that in the building who could have seen something?" Jake asked.

"Yeah, in fact it's a guy I know. He's an ex-cop by the name of Ken McGrew. A real sleaze ball. He got kicked off the force about five years ago for taking bribes from anyone who offered them. Ever since then he's been trying to make a living as a private-eye and security consultant. It's too bad – McGrew was the prototype cool detective...great looking guy, about six-foot-four, real smooth personality. But he's a crook through and through. He's been managing this building as a side deal the past six months; he told me he doesn't get paid squat but gets a rent-free apartment. Knowing Ken

McGrew, he's one of those building managers who peeps at the pretty young co-eds every chance he gets. He always took a shot at the women he brought in for questioning; sometimes he got lucky from what I heard. I questioned McGrew and got the security tapes from him. He says all he saw that night was the bottom of a Jack Daniels bottle."

"Well, I still don't think Harvey is your killer."

"If he's not, I bet he has some idea of who is," Eddie said, "so why don't you take a turn enjoying the splendor of our waiting area and send your boss in? Oh, and here's a tip – under no circumstances would I use the men's room out there. "

Eddie laughed and slapped Jake on the back.

Harvey entered the interview room nervously and sat down to the chair Eddie pointed toward.

Eddie smiled and said, "Mr. Elwood, I'll be straight with you. In my investigation I came across some information that, from some angles, could cast you in a negative light. I want to give you a chance to tell your side of the story, because frankly, I'm a fan of Lincoln State and if we can avoid any publicity that would hurt the athletic program, I would like to do that. But you have to be open and honest with me."

Harvey stayed cool, although he very much wanted to put his face in his hands. He said, "I'm not sure what you're getting at, detective."

"First," Eddie said calmly, "there are rumors circulating that you and Jennifer Stewart had a romantic relationship. Was that the case?"

Harvey sat dead still for a full thirty seconds. Eddie looked into his eyes and didn't blink. Finally, Harvey cracked, "Yes, we have been seeing each other for about a year. But don't make it out to be a sordid affair where I was taking advantage of a young girl. I've never done this sort of thing before and we truly had feelings for each other."

"I am assuming that you are the father of her child," Eddie said, "which could be considered a motive."

Harvey actually rose a few inches from his seat and responded angrily, "No! That's not true! Jennifer and I discussed the baby. I wasn't happy about it, but I certainly wouldn't kill her over that – or anything else."

Eddie said, "Mr. Elwood, I want you to be honest with me... were you at Jennifer Stewart's apartment the night she was killed?"

"Like I told you before, I was home all evening. Alone."

Eddie didn't say a word but just slid the photo across the table. "Is this your car, Mr. Elwood?"

Harvey looked at the photo carefully, "Yes, that is one of my cars. My wife drives that car the majority of the time. I have a Lexus hybrid SUV that I drive almost exclusively. You know, trying to be green. I used Sheila's car to visit Jennifer's apartment once in a while, so my car wouldn't be seen too often in the parking lot of the building. But I wasn't there that night. This photo must be from a different time, but not that night."

Eddie wasn't expecting Harvey to deny that he was at the apartment so convincingly; Eddie thought he would crack when he saw the photo. Could that idiot Ken McGrew have mislabeled the tapes or not turned the recorder on for this entire week? It definitely put a damper on Eddie's certainty that Harvey was there that night.

"Mr. Elwood, I'm not out to embarrass you by making any of this public. I'm trying to work with you on this. But you have to be straight with me. Were you or were you not at the apartment that night?"

Harvey looked like he was ready to begin sobbing, "Detective you've got to believe me, I wasn't there! I was home!"

Eddie had an inspiration, "Did your wife know about the affair? Maybe she went there to confront Jennifer Stewart?"

"Sheila had her suspicions, but I think she would have confronted me rather than go to Jennifer," Harvey said, "Sheila was out that night, but I'm sure it was for a meeting involving some sort of fund-raising cause or another – I looked at her calendar. The only explanation I can think of is that your photo is from the wrong night. I think I drove Sheila's car over there the week before Jennifer was killed."

Eddie was stumped. His gut told him that Harvey was telling the truth. But Ken McGrew would have to be more of a clown than Eddie remembered to make a mistake like that. The security tapes were clearly labeled with the day and date.

Harvey used Eddie's pause to gather some righteous indignation, "Detective, am I a suspect? If not, I am leaving."

Eddie said, "You're free to go, Mr. Elwood. You're not

charged with anything. Thank you for coming in." He walked out to the waiting area and said goodbye to Jake and Harvey.

The door to Harvey's car had barely closed when Harvey said to Jake, "What did the police want with you? What did they ask?"

Jake was ready with an answer, "The detective wanted my opinion as to who Jennifer was friends with at work. Apparently he feels some of the staff have been evasive with him and he knows I'm dating Ellen. He thought he could get me to be more open with him than the women in the office have been. He thought I would have more insight into the office gossip but he was mistaken."

The answer seemed to satisfy Harvey and they made the rest of the short drive in silence.

With the distractions of the week, Jake ignored his duties of preparing for the upcoming football game against the Cincinnati Bearcats. It was a road game for the Abes and Jake was required to make the trip. He decided to make the four-hour drive to Cincinnati on Friday night with Ellen. Jake would wrap up his work duties within a couple hours after Saturday's game and then he and Ellen could spend the rest of the weekend together. Jake and Ellen left for Cincinnati Friday afternoon.

"I'm glad you decided to drive instead of riding the team bus," Ellen said, "it gives us a chance to spend some time together."

"I like that too," Jake said, "but truth be told, I really needed some time away from Harvey and Milt and the whole bunch. It's been a rough week with Harvey. I think the police have connected the dots and figured out his connection to Jennifer. He was in a bad state of mind when we left the police department."

"Do you think he killed Jennifer? It seems like he had a motive. Her pregnancy was obviously going to be a problem for him. Now she's dead – problem solved."

"You know, a week ago I would have said I was one-hundred percent sure that he was innocent. Now I'm not so certain."

They rode in silence for a while. Ellen changed the subject to football.

"Did you see the story in USA Today about the movement to start paying college players?" Ellen asked.

"Yeah, I did. There seems to be a growing call for giving players more than just a scholarship. I'm not sure I agree with that."

"Why not?" Ellen responded, "Colleges make a lot of money from sports. I think it's fair that the athletes should get a little bit of it."

"Athletes do get compensated. They get a free ride on tuition plus room and board. What does that add up to at Lincoln State? Maybe sixty thousand dollars over four years. That's not small change."

Ellen said, "But what about the kids who come from very

poor families? There are lots of costs of college besides tuition, room and board. There's the cost of books, travel and spending money to name a few. That can add up to a few thousand dollars a year, at least. Some families can't afford that."

"But if we start paying athletes, where do you draw the line? How much do you pay them? Let's say we pay all athletes equally, regardless of sport and regardless of gender. Lincoln State has nearly three hundred athletes on scholarship. If we paid each one twenty-five hundred dollars per year that would be a huge chunk out of our budget."

"Maybe only athletes in some sports could be paid," Ellen said, "just the sports that make money."

Jake said, "That would probably be shot down in the courts as illegal, especially if we don't pay women athletes. But even if we could just pay athletes in a few sports, there would be an issue with the definition of an amateur, the athletes would in essence become professionals. Also, it brings up another problem. Is the star quarterback worth more than a benchwarmer? If so, how much more should he get? The whole thing is a huge can of worms."

"OK, OK, I give up!" Ellen laughed, "I've come to the conclusion that I can't win a sports business debate with you."

Jake smiled at Ellen and his mood changed. He began to look forward to a fun weekend.

Chapter Fourteen

The Abes improved their record to six-and-one with a very close win over Cincinnati. Unlike the pattern of their previous wins, Lincoln State didn't jump out to an early lead and let their defense hold the opponent for the rest of the game. Instead, the Abes fell behind by ten points and still trailed by a field goal late in the fourth quarter. But after getting the ball on the fifty-yard line on a fumble by Cincinnati with just two minutes left, Lincoln State's offense was able to score a touchdown with time running out to get the victory.

Slim Haskins, buoyed by the win and another week passing without being contacted by the police, was nothing short of jubilant after the game.

"We have three games left in the conference, two of them at home. If we don't play with our heads up our asses like we did most of today, all three of those games are winnable. We also have the game at Florida in a few weeks. Guys," he said, ignoring the fact that there were four woman reporters in the audience, "I gotta tell you, I'm feeling pretty damned good about playing against Florida."

As usual, Jake handled the scheduling of interviews smoothly. All players and assistant coaches gave perfect interviews – which meant they said little or nothing of substance, but included plenty of clichés and worn-out sound bites that have been spoken thousands of times in post-game interviews. As Jake listened to the answers given by the players, he marveled at why the reporters just didn't stay home and recycle the same quotes from previous post-game interviews. It gave Jake an appreciation for the volatility of Slim Haskins. Like him or not, Slim usually said what was on his mind – often in a colorful and unpredictable way, which was rare in the world of college sports.

By the following Tuesday afternoon, Jake looked back at the trouble-free weekend as the calm before the storm that hit starting on Monday.

An angry Harvey Elwood was on the line when Jake answered his office phone early Monday morning.

"The police just left my house, they confiscated my computers and are heading for my office to take my PC from there," Harvey said, "And the moment the police left, that reporter buddy of yours showed up at my door to ask how I felt about being named a suspect in the Jennifer Stewart murder!"

"Stay calm, Harvey," Jake answered, "I'll see what I can do about Johnny. In the meantime you should stay at home today and avoid the press for now. You're just a suspect, you haven't been arrested. So try not to worry."

"Sheila is pitching a fucking fit," Harvey said, "this was the last piece in the puzzle to confirm her suspicions about my having an affair."

"OK, Harvey. Don't talk to any more reporters. Just sit tight for now and let me call Johnny Rose." With that, Jake hung up.

Jake dialed Johnny's cell phone, "Christ, Johnny! What's going on?"

"The police named Elwood as a suspect. They needed search warrants to get at his phone records and computer files. The only way a judge would go along with it is if they named him in the warrants. That makes it public record. Jake, I don't want to throw the guy under the bus, but I have to report the story. Everybody else will be on this story within a few hours and if I ignore it, I'm not doing my job."

"But this could destroy the athletic program!" Jake said.

"Easy there, my man. I'm not going to report on the affair. That isn't public record and Eddie told me he isn't going to mention it. I think you ought to call Eddie and talk to him, he'll set your mind at ease."

Jake hung up and immediately called Eddie. "Hey, Eddie, it's Jake. What's going on with making Harvey a suspect? Did some other evidence come up?

"No, but last night I got a call from the Chief of Police. He got a call from the mayor. There's gossip all over the city about Harvey and that girl. People are asking the Chief why Elwood hasn't been investigated, implying there's favoritism. The Chief told me in no uncertain terms to name Harvey Elwood as a suspect and start collecting evidence. But don't flip out too much. I see it as a positive thing."

"How do you figure it to be a good thing?" Jake asked, "It seems like a disaster."

"Think about it. We took his computer files and will be looking at his phone records. I figure an important guy like Harvey, if he's telling the truth about being home that night, he just didn't sit there with his thumb up his ass. He had to have done something – surfed the Internet, sent some emails, or maybe he talked to someone on the phone. If so, we can analyze the trail he left, prove he was home and give him an alibi. If he didn't create any evidence that he was at home, then...," Eddie let the sentence trail off.

"I get it," Jake said, "you're either going to clear him or arrest him, depending on what you find. How long will it take to look at his computers and get the phone records?"

"It'll only take a day or so. I'm hoping just like you that we'll find proof that Harvey was home that night. Hell, even if he spent the night looking at porn sites it would save his ass."

Jake felt better after the phone call. Although he had doubts in the corner of his mind, he still refused to believe Harvey was a murderer. But his relief didn't last more than a few hours. Johnny Rose called again Monday afternoon.

"Man, you're not going to believe this," Johnny said, "I stopped in during my lunch hour to visit Jackie Jefferson – he's the tattoo artist of choice for the local brothers – and I see he's got an autographed football and a couple of auto-graphed Lincoln State jerseys sitting there in his shop. I ask him where he got the stuff. He reluctantly admits that some of the Lincoln State players traded him autographed stuff in exchange for free tattoos."

The phone almost slipped from Jake's fingers. He screamed, "What? That's a serious violation of NCAA rules!"

"It gets worse. Jackie says they've been doing this for the past year or so. You know how it is with tatts, man. You get one and the next day you start thinking about getting the next one. They're addicting. Anyway, Jackie's been selling the stuff online. Trying to make a few extra bucks, you know? He normally doesn't leave the stuff sitting out in the open in his shop but he happened to have a buyer coming in later today."

"Oh no," is all Jake could utter.

"You know what they say in the infomercials...*But wait, there's even more!* Doing fine tattoos isn't the only business Jackie runs from that shop. He also does a fair amount of bookmak-ing, and – just between you and me – sells a little weed. Jackie did time at Joliet prison a few years back."

"Let me get this straight. We have football players selling autographs to a drug dealing, convicted felon who runs a bookie operation out of a downtown tattoo parlor."

"You're very quick, Jake. I don't understand why everybody says you're not too bright."

"Very funny. Who are the players?"

"Not too hard to figure that out. I looked at the merchandise. The autographs were from Logan Williams, Jimmy Jackson and Lavelle Smith."

Jake felt a twinge of guilt when his first thought was that none of the players Johnny mentioned were irreplaceable. All three were starters but not stars on the team. "This is going to be a nightmare. And it's coming right on top of the thing with Harvey. I gotta go." The phone clicked loudly in Johnny's ear.

After he got off the phone with Johnny, Jake went immediately to the compliance office. Like all NCAA Division I sports programs, Lincoln State had a person who was responsible for nothing other than studying and enforcing the overwhelming set of rules established by the NCAA. Joe Manning was an attorney, which was almost a necessity given the complexity and legal implications of managing a compliance office.

Jake sat down in Joe Manning's sparse office. It was bleak and plain, with gray walls and very few personal items on display. When Joe Manning had someone in his office, he obviously didn't want the visitor to feel comfortable.

"Joe, I just became aware of some major shit." Jake repeated Johnny's story.

"Holy crap!" Joe Manning said, "We have to launch an internal investigation immediately, and of course, inform the NCAA. As you know, the NCAA expects colleges to police themselves to a great degree. If we gather the facts and take appropriate action, Lincoln State can hopefully minimize the long-term damage to the program."

"What do you mean by long-term damage?"

"Things like having the NCAA take away some of our scholarships for several years. Or they may strip the school of championships involving the guilty players. In extreme cases they could even suspend one or more of our sports."

Jake asked, "What's the timing going to be? We have a month left in the football season."

"The first thing we need to do is suspend the three players, probably for the rest of the regular season. We can do that without any hard evidence. The next question is: what did Slim Haskins know about this? And if he knew, for how long was he aware of it? Getting to the bottom of this mess will take a while. There definitely won't be an impact other than the three suspensions during the regular season. But if we make it to a bowl game and there's more to this story than we know about right now, the shit may hit the fan before the beginning of January."

Tuesday afternoon, Eddie Martin called Harvey, who was still hiding at home. "Mr. Elwood, I have good news. After analyzing your phone and computer records, we can definitely place you in your home for the entire evening. You have been officially dropped as a suspect. I'd like to offer my sincere apologies for any embarrassment that this caused you."

Harvey was in no mood to accept an apology. The last twenty-four hours had been a nightmare of pretending not to be home to duck reporters and listening to Sheila scream at him until she stormed out of the house. He hadn't seen her since, but she would be back. It was a worse punishment to have Sheila *not* divorce him, and she knew it.

"This did cause me great embarrassment, detective. I can't help but think it could have been avoided."

"As painful as it was, it was the most expedient way to separate you from the case," Eddie explained, "the media didn't make any direct accusations about your affair, all they could do was mention that there were unsubstantiated rumors. If this had dragged on it could have ended up being much worse for you, trust me."

Well, one problem was out of the way, Harvey thought. Now he had this autographs-for-tattoos mess to deal with that Joe Manning had called him about a couple of hours before. Harvey was still wearing a bathrobe at three o'clock and headed for the bathroom to take his first shower in nearly three days. He sighed. It was time to get back to work.

Slim Haskins walked into his office after practice and found Joe Manning sitting in his chair typing on his computer keyboard. "What the fuck are you doing?" he asked rudely.

"Coach, we have it on good authority that three of your players have been selling autographed Lincoln State memorabilia. These same players have been consorting with a convicted felon who runs an illegal gambling operation. Please bring Logan Williams, James Jackson and Lavelle Smith into your office immediately."

The three players caved within minutes and, while they admitted guilt about the tattoos, all claimed ignorance of the rules and swore they didn't know Jackie was a bookie or ex-con. They were informed of their suspensions and told to report to the compliance office the following morning to answer additional questions. After they had left, Joe Manning asked, "What was your knowledge of this activity?"

"I didn't know a thing until just now," Slim Haskins said defensively, "if I knew anything was going on I would have reported it, of course."

Without permission or a greeting, one of Joe Manning's assistants suddenly appeared in Slim's office, sat down and started making copies of his computer files. The investigation had officially begun.

Between Harvey's situation and the player suspensions, the rest of the week was a blur for Jake. He was on the phone or talking in person to reporters virtually every waking minute. Lincoln State's winning streak had vaulted the Abes into the national spotlight. Besides the usual Springfield press, reporters were now calling from Chicago, Indianapolis and St. Louis. Camera crews from ESPN and the big TV stations in Chicago showed up unannounced at odd hours. Ellen was very helpful, bringing Jake food, since he was trapped in the athletic offices for all but a few hours each day.

It was already Friday morning and Jake hadn't even thought about his preparation work for the upcoming road game against the Texas El-Paso Miners. It didn't really matter, because the TV and Internet were too packed with titillating stories about Harvey and what was being called the "autographs-for-tattoos scandal" to have room for any positive news about the football team. Not that there was anything to report. Slim Haskins had put his team into a virtual lockdown; coaches and players were barred from speaking to reporters and practices were closed to the media.

Finally, at 7 o'clock Friday night, Jake couldn't take it anymore. He called Ellen and suggested a late dinner.

As they were having dessert, Ellen said, "Do you have enough energy to...you know...go back to your apartment after we're finished here?"

"Of course, I've been waiting all week," Jake said, and reached over to squeeze Ellen's hand.

Jake made love to Ellen as if it would be their last time. It was long and thorough, with no part of her body left unexplored.

"Wow, that was amazing," Ellen whispered.

"The way things have been going, I don't know when we'll have time to get together again. So I wanted to make the most of it."

They laid in silence for a minute. Then Ellen said, "Listen Jake. I don't want to spoil the mood, but I have to tell you something I've been thinking about since I heard about those players getting suspended. I may have accidentally overheard Slim Haskins talking about it to someone a while ago."

"When did this happen?"

"It was about a month ago. I was filling in for the football office receptionist who called in sick. This guy came in, he was a booster. I could hear him and Haskins talking. I just heard fragments, but now with this news about an investigation, what they were saying fits in with the facts. I heard the booster say, "players can't be associating with gamblers" and a few other things.

"Holy crap," Jake said, "I think you better talk to Joe Manning on Monday. But in the meantime, let's make the most of tonight. I'm not through with you yet."

Chapter Fifteen

Eddie set up another meeting with the apartment building manager, Ken McGrew. Those security tapes could be a big help, Eddie thought, if only the security system worked right. When he reviewed the tapes a couple of days earlier, he was in a hurry and focusing only on anything to do with Harvey Elwood. Now that Elwood was cleared, every second of every tape needed to be reviewed in excruciating detail. The next couple of days were going to be a grind.

McGrew's apartment was a typical bachelor's residence and exactly what Eddie expected from Ken McGrew – a complete mess, littered with empty fast food wrappers, beer bottles and half-full glasses. A recliner in the center of the room, obviously McGrew's home base, looked like an island of garbage. If McGrew had a vacuum cleaner, he apparently didn't know it had to be plugged in and turned on in order to work, because Eddie had seen cleaner parking lots. Various security gear was spread around the small living room – cameras, editing equipment, recorders and other items.

"Glad you cleaned up the place for me, Ken," Eddie said as he walked in.

"Hey, I have other priorities. A lot of things are going on in my life right now," McGrew shot back defensively.

"Do you have the tapes for me?"

"Yeah, here they are" said McGrew, pointing to a large cardboard box, "Right after the killing, I stopped re-using the tapes because I figured you would need them. I got the building owner to reimburse me and bought thirty new ones. Man, he was pissed about spending seventy stinking bucks. Plus, do you know how hard it is to buy VHS tapes these days?"

"A new security system may not be a waste of money," Eddie said.

McGrew ignored the comment, "So, how are things at the department?"

The last thing Eddie wanted was to be buddies with this asshole, but it might be helpful to get McGrew talking freely, "Same old shit. What's going on with you? Someday I may want to leave the force, so tell me – how's the private security business?"

"It's tough, but it can be rewarding at times. Just like when I was on the police force, you run into a lot of women. I'm banging this good looking old broad right now. She hired me to follow her husband, thought he was fooling around and she was right. I broke the bad news to her; she got pissed and wanted some revenge sex. Of course, I was happy to oblige."

"You're a real prince," Eddie said sarcastically.

"I take what I can get. This broad, though, is different. She actually likes me – she's high society, I think she digs me cause I'm, you know, rough around the edges. And she is loaded. I'm definitely trying to get something long-term going with her, talk her into divorcing her husband and getting a big settlement. If she does that, I'll be sitting in butter."

Eddie blinked, trying to erase the image of Ken McGrew's middle-aged bottom coated in yellow, slippery liquid.

McGrew went on, "Plus I have another deal I'm working on that could lead to some very nice money. When an opportunity presents itself in this business you have to know when to grab it by the balls and that's what I'm going to do."

Eddie suddenly had enough of Ken McGrew. He stood up and said, "Show me the security system again. I want to see exactly how it works."

***

Joe Manning, the compliance officer for Lincoln State, listened to Ellen describe the conversation she overheard between Slim Haskins and the booster.

"I need every word that you overheard, exactly as you remember it," Manning said.

"I know it's important...but it was a month ago, September twentieth, I checked the date. At the time, it didn't seem important. It completely slipped my mind, I forgot all about it. Then when this all came up a few days ago, I started to think about it."

"What do you remember?"

"A man came into the football office. The coach was expecting him but there was nothing in the appointment log. He was dressed in a nice suit; you could tell it was expensive. Good looking tall guy, over six feet in his late forties, a little gray but mostly dark hair. He looked like a lawyer or a business executive. The door was slightly open to the coach's office so I caught some of what they were saying. The guy says something like, 'you need to be aware of this,' and then after a while I hear him say, 'known in the criminal community,' and 'you need to keep those kids away from him.'"

"Anything else you can think of?"

"Coach Haskins was really irritated and said something like, 'I know, I know. I'll take care of it,' something like that, as the guy was walking out."

"Any other things you remember about the visitor? What makes you think he's a booster?"

"He mentioned something about giving a lot of money to the program," Ellen said, "and he said he didn't want anything screwing up the good season Lincoln State was having."

"You have no idea who this visitor was?"

"The guy wasn't particularly happy when he left. I said good-bye to him as he was walking out but he didn't answer or even look at me when he blew by my desk. He was very rude. That's all I can remember. Sorry," Ellen apologized.

Joe Manning thanked Ellen and she left his office. He had the date it happened and a description of the visitor. The next step was to review his list of boosters to find all the major contributors who were lawyers and business people working in the Springfield area. There couldn't be too many. He could also confront Slim Haskins with the basic facts and hope that his bluff worked and Haskins revealed the name of the booster.

If Haskins knew about the problem and ignored it, or tried to handle it himself, there was going to be a major problem. The NCAA requires schools to report potential problems and launch a probe, which Lincoln State was now doing. Also, the coach's contract had a specific clause requiring him to report any potential violations immediately to the compliance office. If Haskins knew something and didn't report it, he might be having the best season of his career, but it would be his last one at Lincoln State. Joe Manning would make sure the investigation took a long time to complete, at least until after the regular season, and maybe even after the bowl game.

***

Johnny broke the autographs-for-tattoos story in his column and was running an investigation of his own into who was involved and whether Slim Haskins was pulling a cover-up. Other media, including the big Midwest papers and national cable sports networks, were scouring Springfield for information as well. Jake agreed to meet Johnny for lunch at D'Arcy's Pint.

After they settled into their table away from the rest of the lunch crowd, Johnny said, "Man, this is wild. Look across the way, sitting over by the window. Those guys are from ESPN. There are so many sports reporters hanging around in Springfield the past two days that we're tripping over each other's schlongs."

"Somebody is going to find out something with all the digging going on. Have you learned anything new?"

"There are definitely rumors flying. I've been to half the car dealers in a twenty-mile radius and nobody will come right out with it – but some of the car salesmen I talked to are telling me that a number of Lincoln State players got really sweet deals on cars in the past few years – too sweet to be legitimate. You go into the sales manager's office and more often than not, there's autographed pictures of an Abes player or two on their wall. That's not a crime in and of itself but it makes you wonder."

"But it boils down to what Slim Haskins knew, and when he knew it. I have to tell you something about that." Jake relayed Ellen's story about Slim's conversation with the mysterious visitor to his office.

"What you have there is the smoking gun," Johnny said, "but for me to take it to my editor, I have to find this mystery man. You can help me out by getting me a list of major contributors to Lincoln State athletics. I know that's public record but you can get it much quicker than I can. If we can narrow the possibilities down to some reasonable number, I can go out and shake the bushes and see what falls out. Who else knows about this?"

"Just Joe Manning, Ellen and me," Jake answered, "You can trust Ellen and me to keep quiet, but when Joe Manning starts calling boosters it's likely to get out."

"Jake, Jake, Jake," Johnny shook his head, "you shock me with your naivety. How fast do you think Joe Manning is going to move on this thing? He'll drag his feet like he's wearing cement loafers. Secretly, he's probably pissed off that Ellen came forward with information because it requires him to take some action sooner than he'd like. Otherwise, Manning would be finding a million other things to do with his time. He doesn't want to dig up any dirt on Haskins until the dust has settled from this season."

"But with all these reporters hanging around the city, won't somebody find something pretty soon?"

"Maybe, and that's why I'm looking too. If this thing turns ugly, I want to be the one who finds the dirt. I suspect these reporters won't be here long, a couple more days and they'll move onto the next story somewhere else. As far as the official school investigation, I can tell you for a fact how it's going to happen: Manning has already reported the three players to the NCAA. Those kids are history as far as ever playing college football again, so the school is off the hook for the time being. Manning will drag his feet and keep his fingers crossed Haskins didn't know what was going on. If it turns out Haskins knew anything at all, the school will throw him under the bus. Everyone is expendable in these things, and the administration will kill as many sacrificial lambs as they need to in order to protect the program.

"Sounds harsh," Jake said.

"Welcome to college athletics," Johnny replied.

***

Slim Haskins sat alone in his office with the scouting report for the next opponent, New Mexico State. The binder was still unopened; he was having difficulty concentrating on anything other than the shit storm of problems in his life that seemed to be multiplying daily. Every time his phone rang or there was a knock on his office door, he envisioned the worst possible scenario. Sometimes he was certain it was the police with an arrest warrant, other times he was sure it would be Joe Manning or Harvey Elwood, accompanied by campus security, to toss him from the athletic department forever.

His stress level was beyond what he ever imagined possible. For years, Slim had dreamt of what a season like this would be like – national media attention and the importance of every game magnified by ten-fold. In his countless fantasies, there was never a dark cloud in the sky. Now he was living the real thing, only it seemed more like a surrealistic nightmare than the season he had long dreamed of.

Some of this could have been avoided, he thought regretfully. He knew already last spring about this crap that the media was now calling "autographs-for-tattoos." He chose to ignore it, even after that lawyer came to visit him last month.

The shitty thing was that those three asshole players were expendable; they were good, but not irreplaceable. The coach still had this week to get the replacements ready, and New Mexico State was anything but a powerhouse – the Abes could probably beat them with their second string. The following week against still-undefeated Florida was another story. Haskins had to have the team running on all cylinders for that game.

It was incredible how things were falling into place for the Abes and their chances to make a major bowl, or even the national title game. The major college power teams were falling like dominoes; if the Abes could beat Florida, they could end up playing for the national title. The thought being hoisted off the field on the shoulders of his players while holding the championship trophy over his head brought a smile to his face for the first time in weeks. Slim pushed the binder aside and grabbed a pad of paper. He told his assistant head coach to call a team meeting – he was going to have a heart-to-heart talk with his football team.

Chapter Sixteen

The football locker room door was closed and locked, and every nook carefully checked to make sure no one except players and coaches were in the area. The players sat in street clothes, having been summoned to practice a half-hour early.

Slim Haskins stood in the middle of the locker room floor with an air of confidence and authority. His speech would be a combination of carefully drafted and memorized lines and words that he hoped would flow directly from his emotions.

"Gentlemen, the football program is under attack. A few of your teammates made a mistake and now the media is looking at Lincoln State football like a shark looks at a sick fish. They are looking for the kill; they want to ruin the successful season that each and every one of you have worked so hard to achieve."

The coach paused for dramatic effect and let his gaze slowly sweep around the locker room and meet every player's eye for a moment or two.

"Our own administration has even turned on us," he continued. "Everyone in this room is under scrutiny – not just by the media but by our own athletic department! There is an investigation going on and it is serious. We could end up forfeiting games and losing the dream that we've all been striving for. Who knows, some of you personally may be kicked to the curb like your three teammates were."

Haskins paused again, and looked around the room. He saw a mixture of fear and anger on the players' faces, exactly the emotions he had hoped for. It was time to move on to the second part of his speech.

"From this moment forward, we need to be united – and I mean one-hundred percent united; every single person in this room. First thing: Every one of you needs to read the NCAA rules. If you need a book, see Coach Simpson and he'll give you one. We're going to schedule a review session within the next week and expect every damn player will pay close attention to what is said and follow the rules. Second: We will no longer speak a single word about anything that happens off the field to the media. Not one word. From anyone. We will answer questions about what happens on the football field because we have to. But any question that involves anything else will either be ignored or answered with 'no comment.' Are we all in agreement about this? If not, now is the time to talk about it."

Nearly one-hundred heads bobbed up and down in unison. So far so good, Haskins thought.

"We are on the verge of achieving our greatest dreams. This team has what it takes to make it to the big game. But we have to be united as never before. The media is one thing, but our own administration has not only turned their back on us, they're trying to dig up dirt. We must show a united front, gentlemen. Their investigation has to find nothing! Unfortunately, we have to sacrifice the college careers of three fine players for the greater good. But our position with the administration is that we knew nothing and no one else participated in this business that caused all the trouble. If you have anything in your possession that could be called into question in a university investigation, now is the time to rid yourself of it. Look at your emails, your texts, or any of that crap and clean it up. If you can't document paying for a car, stereo system or anything else then get rid of it. You will do your best to appear cooperative with the compliance office, but our position is that no one in this room has been guilty of any wrongdoing and no one knows anything about anyone else."

Now that he had said what needed to be said, he needed to drive the point home.

"If any of you don't want to help your team form a united front, it will be noted by the coaching staff. The team comes before any individual, and anyone who does not completely demonstrate a team attitude will find themselves losing playing time and possibly not having their scholarship renewed. Are we all clear on this?"

Again, every head in the room nodded in agreement and there were quite a few mumbled affirmations. Haskins said, "OK, let's get dressed and head out to the field."

***

Ken McGrew sat alone in his old, beat-up sedan, parked in the athletic department parking lot, waiting for football practice to end. He had parked there the previous day as well and noted which car Slim Haskins drove off in. He watched the players leave, walking out of the football area in small groups. About an hour later, the coaches started to come out of the building and another hour later McGrew saw Slim Haskins walk out into the parking lot. Ken McGrew intercepted the coach while Haskins was ten yards from his car.

"Coach, we haven't met but I need to talk to you about an urgent matter," McGrew said.

"Sorry, it's been a long day. Set up interviews through Jake Goodman in the Sports Information office."

"This is a personal matter, an important personal matter."

"Listen, mister; I don't know you, so get away from me." Haskins glanced around the parking lot. It was an hour past dusk and the lot was well lit, but he saw no one else in the area.

"This involves Jennifer Stewart. I think you've heard of her."

Slim Haskins had brushed by McGrew, but stopped and turned. He tried to hide the worry from his face and appear nonchalant. "Yeah, that girl who got killed...so what about her?"

"I have something you need to listen to," McGrew said, pulled out a tiny recorder and pressed the play button. McGrew played about fifteen seconds of the tape containing the threatening discussion Haskins had with Jennifer Stewart. Even in the dark under just the parking lot lights, McGrew saw the coach's face turn pale.

"Where did you get that? Who the fuck are you?"

"Good questions," McGrew said. "Can we finish this conversation in your car? It's getting cold. This wind is a killer."

Haskins looked around the empty parking lot once more and clicked the remote to unlock his car doors. He got in and started the engine.

McGrew continued, "I manage the apartment building where Jennifer Stewart lived. There's a lot of security in that building. I have you on camera coming in and going out. I have this recording and I have other evidence as well." McGrew actually had nothing but the recording, but he thought his plan would be more effective if he bluffed that he had more evidence.

Slim Haskins slumped in the passenger seat; he looked like a defeated man. "All right. What do you want?"

"I have it on good authority that you have in your possession photos of Harvey Elwood and Jennifer Stewart in a sexually compromising position. I want you to give me the photo files on one of those little USB drives. Then I expect you to delete any printed copies and files that you have of those photos. You will not use these photos against Harvey Elwood in any way and if you try, I will send the recording and other evidence to the police."

Haskins sat up a little straighter. Was that all that the guy wanted? He had given up on the idea of using the photos anyway. With the season the football team was having there was no point risking blackmail. And if this tattoo deal blew up in his face, he would probably be fired anyway and there was nothing Harvey Elwood could do to save him. Maybe he was going to get off the hook after all.

Slim's relief didn't last long as McGrew continued, "I also want the sum of one hundred thousand dollars. Payable in cash, within one week."

"Impossible!" screamed Haskins, "This is the middle of the football season. I work a hundred hours a week and we have a game in less than three days. That's going to take a lot of doing. There's no way I can round up that kind of money."

"OK then, you got until a week from this Friday to get the money. But give me those photo files tomorrow. I'll be here in the parking lot at the same time as tonight. Here's some advice, Haskins – don't fuck with me. You try to pull anything with those photos and I'll make sure you end up in prison for the rest of your life." Ken McGrew got out of the car and stood in the parking lot until Slim Haskins drove off.

***

Jake grabbed the large envelope containing a printout of the top fifty Lincoln State athletic boosters and headed out of the office to meet Johnny in their new favorite spot. He found Johnny sitting in the same remote table in a distant corner of the pub.

"I see we're sitting at 'our table' again, darling," Jake said as he sat down.

"You're a frigging riot," Johnny said, "I like the privacy. Most of the competition has blown town already but there are still a few guys hanging around looking for dirt. We don't need anybody eavesdropping."

"You're right, but try to relax. You look like crap; you're stressed out."

"I know, buddy, I am stressed out to the max. Lincoln State is my home turf and I don't want any of those other clowns getting a story ahead of me. If there's something more to this scandal, which I hope there isn't, I want to be the one who breaks it. So do you have the list?"

"Yeah, I have a list of the top fifty contributors. The biggest is three hundred thousand last year and number fifty gave about ten thousand. They're almost all male, only six are female, so that doesn't narrow things down much. Eighteen of them are located out of state, which I think eliminates them."

"I'm with you so far, that leaves twenty-six," Johnny said.

"I had Ellen do some additional checking online and out of the twenty-six, eleven are retired and elderly so that cuts the number to fifteen."

"Now we're getting somewhere."

"We can eliminate my dad, he's one of the fifteen," Jake said.

"Good thinking, Einstein," Johnny said.

"Ellen found that four of the fourteen are lawyers, partners in law firms in the city. Five are business owners or executives who would be likely to wear suits."

Johnny piped in, "That makes nine people we need to see. Didn't Ellen say that the guy was forty-ish, dark hair with a touch of gray, average build, no glasses? All we have to do is visit these nine guys and see what they look like. If they match the description, we'll chat them up and see what they tell us."

"We can't just drop in on these guys out of the blue."

"I'm a reporter, man. Dropping in on people is what I do. Here's the plan: you lead the way, you tell them you are stopping by to express the university's appreciation for their donation. You forget, Jake, you're a little bit of a celebrity around here. Personally I don't see why, but you are. Then we tell them I'm tagging along for a story I'm doing about you. It's simple – we won't even need to wear fake moustaches or wigs," Johnny laughed.

The first three visits were fruitless; none of the three men matched Ellen's description of the mystery booster. The fourth visit was to the law firm of Harris and Smith, LLC and from a visual comparison to Ellen's description, attorney Robert Smith looked like their man.

After ten minutes of chit-chat and Jake's effusive thanks for Mr. Smith's donations to the athletic program, Johnny steered the conversation to the three suspended players.

"Do you think the football team will miss those three starters?" Johnny asked Robert Smith.

"Maybe not for the New Mexico State game this week, but definitely against Florida," Smith answered.

Jake zoomed in and said, "You know, there are rumors circulating that Coach Haskins was aware of the problem several months before it became public."

As an attorney, Robert Smith was skilled at hiding his emotions. But both Johnny and Jake saw the instantaneous surprise flash across Smith's face. Jake continued, "It was supposedly a booster who brought it to Slim Haskin's attention."

There was a long, uncomfortable silence, finally broken by Robert Smith. "Gentlemen, I appreciate your visit. I've been a loyal alumnus of Lincoln State for nearly twenty years. And I've seen enough years of us being pushed around on the football field. This year is special."

Smith got up from his chair, walked to his office door and closed it. He sat down and continued, "About a month ago, I had what I consider a very informal discussion with Coach Haskins. I was simply passing along a rumor I heard. It was all hearsay, and there is absolutely no written or email communication with the coach about this matter."

Jake said, "Surely you don't want this issue to damage the

school. You've been around long enough to realize that the entire athletic program could be in jeopardy if NCAA rules were violated and we don't punish the guilty parties. Are you willing to live with that responsibility?"

The point of the question was clear to all three men. Jake was asking Smith if he knew of any hard evidence that could arise in the future and incriminate Haskins.

"Informal conversations are not evidence," Smith said, "and there was absolutely nothing beyond that. So I think there is nothing more to talk about regarding that matter. On another subject, Jake...what are my chances of getting a couple of tickets to the game at Florida?"

"I'll certainly see what I can do, Mr. Smith," Jake smiled, "but I have a feeling that after this weekend there'll be lots of people asking that same question."

Johnny and Jake left Smith's office and pushed the elevator button for the first floor. As the elevator door closed, Johnny said, "It looks like Slim Haskins is off the hook on this one."

"I guess so," Jake answered, "if there isn't any trail of evidence that Haskins knew about what those players were doing, the damage stops with the three suspensions. It's obvious that he knew something but either didn't take it seriously or he decided to bury it, but there's no proof."

"Yeah. I got to tell you Jake, I've been reporting on the football team for a while now, and Slim Haskins has got to be the luckiest guy on the planet with the shit he's gotten away with over the years."

Across town in the football offices, Slim Haskins didn't feel lucky in the slightest. He was scrambling to come up with a hundred thousand dollars and preparing for his encounter that evening with Ken McGrew.

Chapter Seventeen

While the Lincoln State equipment managers busily packed for the trip to play the New Mexico State Aggies, Slim Haskins was preparing to meet again with Ken McGrew. He had a USB drive containing the explicit photos of Harvey and Jennifer, and if McGrew pressed him on the issue, Haskins would report that the wheels were in motion to have the cash in hand by the following week.

Slim Haskins thought long and hard trying to understand the situation. Apparently, this McGrew character managed the building where Jennifer lived and there were various security systems in place. Somehow he had gotten the recording he played, and hinted there was other evidence, whatever the hell that could be. There was a chance he was bluffing about the other stuff, but Slim figured the recording alone was probably enough to land him in prison. He was in the girl's apartment that night and once the cops had a suspect they might be able to do something with his DNA. He was convinced Jennifer was alive and not mortally wounded when he left her, but that would be almost impossible to prove. A hundred grand was not an insignificant sum, but if it would get this guy off his back, Slim Haskins would pay it.

The locker room was empty, the coaches and players all gone for the night. Right now there were still some student equipment managers loading the trailer, but they were too exhausted to care what was going on anywhere except between the equipment storage room and the semi-trailer. The truck was nearly full of Lincoln State football gear and would leave in an hour or two to make the twenty-hour journey to Las Cruces. The team and coaches would take a charter plane on Friday afternoon. With the football parking lot empty and dark, it was a good time and place to meet McGrew.

Trying to duplicate his actions of the previous evening, Slim Haskins trudged slowly toward his car. Sure enough, a 1990 Oldsmobile sedan pulled into the lot and parked next to Slim's car. McGrew got out, turned up the collar of a decrepit trench coat and approached the coach.

McGrew was all business. "You got it?" he said flatly.

Slim Haskins couldn't help but think that McGrew sounded like a detective in a bad 1940s movie, "Yeah, here are the photo files. For all you know, I still have copies of the files."

"Hey, if you're that hard up for jerk-off material, feel free to use them," McGrew retorted. "Just remember, if the photos ever become public the recording I have goes straight to the cops. What about the cash?"

"I'm working on it," Haskins said irritably, "You'll have it next week."

"Good. I'll be here next Thursday, same time. Make the payment in hundreds, put it in a nice Lincoln State duffle bag. And I will count it so don't try to pull any shit."

"Hundreds? For fuck sake, what bank in this town is going to give me a thousand hundreds? Open a bank account with an out-of-town bank and I'll make a transfer. It'll leave a paper trail but it won't get the whole fucking town talking about why the football coach needs a hundred grand in cash. You should know that. What kind of lousy blackmailer are you?"

"I'll think about it," McGrew said as he got into his car and drove off, leaving Slim Haskins standing alone in the dark parking lot, wondering if paying off this idiot dirt bag was the right course of action.

Inspired by the coach's speech earlier that week, the Lincoln State Abes came out against the Aggies with fire in their eyes. A large contingent of traveling Lincoln State fans saw their team score early and often. The score was 20-0 Lincoln State at the end of the first quarter. With a fifty-five point lead, Slim Haskins started emptying the bench with ten minutes left in the game. The final score was Lincoln State 64, New Mexico State 3.

The visitor's locker room was jubilant as Jake walked through. He made his way to the media room to gather requests from the press of which coaches and players were wanted for interviews. The player most in demand was Onolulo Kahona, the Samoan defensive lineman. Since the UCLA game, Kahona had terrorized opponents and was the reason that the Abes had one of the leading defenses in the nation. Earlier in the week, the nominations for the major college football awards were announced and Onolulo Kahona was one of four nominees for the Bronko Nagurski Award, which was given to the outstanding defensive player in the land. No Lincoln State football player had been nominated for a major national award since the playing days of Harvey Elwood, over thirty years before.

As usual, Slim Haskins started the press conference with a rundown of his version of the game and a question and answer session.

The first question came from Johnny Rose, "Coach, what are your feelings about the chance for a major bowl or even a trip to the national title game?"

"You know the policy on that sort of thing, we take it one game at a time. But it's only human to look at the rankings. Lincoln State was ranked sixteenth in the country going into this game. We probably won't move much if everyone ahead of us wins this week. Next week we have Tulsa at home, not a bad team. And then the week after that we play at Florida. We wrap up against Iowa State. If we win them all, we deserve to get into a major bowl game. If things fall the right way, we could have a shot at the big game. If we don't win our remaining games, we don't deserve to go anywhere. Simple as that."

A television reporter who traveled from Chicago asked, "Did you miss the three suspended players in this game?"

Haskins' eyes showed some anger but he kept his composure, "No, but I'd love to have those three guys back. Personally I think they got a raw deal from the administration and that's all I'll say about that. Their replacements stepped up and played great. I expect they will continue to do that for the remaining three games."

Johnny couldn't help himself and piped in, "Do you really think those three players didn't deserve to be kicked off the team?"

"I said what I have to say about that subject, Mr. Rose," Haskins fumed, "Take it how you like."

"Your history as coach at Lincoln State is filled with players violating not only school policies but NCAA rules. I think it's a valid question to ask about your attitude regarding how your players conduct themselves."

The room became perfectly still and the air hung thick with tension. After ten seconds of silence, Slim Haskins said, "No more questions. I'm going back to the locker room." And with that he turned and walked out the media room door.

Jake quickly stepped up to the vacant podium and glared at Johnny. "I'm sure Onolulo Kahona will be here in a few moments. In the meantime, I'll hand out some press information provided by the Bronko Nagurski Award committee."

A half-dozen interviews later, the press conference was over. As the media members were filing out, Jake approached Johnny Rose.

"What was that all about with you and Haskins?" Jake asked.

"I'm sorry I lost it, buddy. Remember, you were gone from Springfield for the past four years. I've put up with that man's shit for all that time. I know he's trying to be loyal to his players but they got caught red-handed. He needs to act like a head coach of a Division I college football program and be accountable for how his players act off the field."

"I get it, Johnny. But there's a time and place."

"Listen, Jake. I'm all for the Abes having a dream season. Christ, we deserve to be in the spotlight for a change. But I'm going to do my job."

"You're right. However, you just made my job harder. I'm going to have to talk with Haskins to keep him from blacklisting you. If he cuts you off from the players you won't have anything to write about. And he's very pissed off right now."

Johnny broke out a broad grin. "I know you'll go to bat for me with him, pal. Sorry I made things hard on you. But I'll go to sleep tonight knowing I did the right thing today."

"I know. Don't worry about Haskins. I'll schmooze him on the flight back to Springfield tomorrow morning. Plus remind him that he can't afford to cut you off from the players. You're the number one sports guy in the Springfield area and everyone knows it."

"Thanks, buddy, I'd blush but you'd never notice the difference. In the meantime, how about seeing how much damage we can do to Las Cruces tonight?"

As Jake promised, he was able to soothe Slim Haskins' feelings toward Johnny Rose. Johnny called Jake first thing Monday morning and suggested that he and Jake meet with Eddie. The police investigation was stalled once again and Eddie was looking for any leads that Jake or Johnny might be able to provide.

The trio met at Popeye's Barbeque for lunch on Tuesday. As usual, Jake found Eddie and Johnny in a remote booth.

"Where did you come up with this place?" Jake asked Johnny.

"Hey, you're lunching with a cop and a reporter. We never get confused with Bill Gates in the income department. Popeye's is the best barbeque in this part of the state. You can get top-notch ribs and a Diet Pepsi and still get change back from a ten. You ought to bring that girl of yours here and show her you got real taste."

Jake suddenly thought about Ellen. With all the stuff that had been happening when did he talk to her last? "You're the gourmet, Johnny. I'll take your word for it."

As they munched on ribs, fries and coleslaw, Eddie said, "I've got two people looking at the tapes from the victim's apartment building and it's painstaking work. We're looking thirty days times twenty-four hours. You can fast forward some but you have to pay close attention. And...."

Eddie paused and looked up. Standing at their table was Ken McGrew, who said, "Well, you never know who you'll bump into. Howdy, detective. How are those tapes coming along?"

"Slow, as you can imagine. I'll get them back to you when we're done with them. Ken McGrew, this is Jake Goodman from the Lincoln State athletic department and reporter John Rose of the *State Journal-Register*."

"Jake Goodman, huh? I had some dealings with your old man a few years back. Turned me down for a job as head of security for his company after I left the police force."

Jake gave no response. With one glance, Jake could see why his father didn't hire McGrew. The guy was wearing a beat up polyester suit with a ten-year-old tie, topped off with a wrinkled trench coat. He looked like a sloppier version of that disheveled TV detective that Peter Falk played. Johnny couldn't contain his reporter instincts and asked, "If you'll forgive my poetry, so Mr. McGrew...what is it that you do?"

"I'm an independent security consultant; I've done a bit of work for Harvey Elwood, background checks on prospective hires like this kid here," McGrew winked lewdly at Jake, "and I'm also in charge of security for the building where that coed was murdered."

"Well, keep up the good work keeping your building safe," Johnny said sarcastically, "nice meeting you."

Ken McGrew took the dismissal in stride, smiled and walked away.

"What's with that asshole?" Johnny asked Eddie.

"Forget about him," Eddie said, "let's talk about the case. Like I said, we're looking at the security tapes and so far have found nothing. And I've been running all over your fine campus talking to everyone I can think of. The victim's teachers, classmates...you name it and I've talked to them. My boss is really on my ass because of this case. No matter where I look, I keep coming back to the athletic department, Jake. I still think Harvey Elwood is somehow involved in this. I don't know what the connection is but there's something going on there."

"What would you like me to do? In case you don't recall, I'm the Sports Information Director for the hottest college football story in the country right now. I haven't talked to my girlfriend in four, maybe five, days. I don't even remember. Luckily there hasn't been a scandal in the athletic program in one whole week so I've been getting five hours of sleep a night instead of two or three, but who knows what tomorrow will bring?"

Johnny said, "I think what Eddie's asking is that you buddy up a little more with Harvey Elwood. He likes you, Jake, and he trusts you. If he's got something on his mind, I think you're as good a bet as anyone to be the person he'll confide in."

"Fair enough, I'll see what I can do," Jake said.

When Jake got back to the office, he picked up his phone and dialed Ellen's extension. She picked up and said, "Who is this calling? A stranger from my distant past?"

"Hopefully your immediate future if you'll have dinner with me tonight."

"Sure, why not? But you better pick me up. If we meet somewhere I'm not sure I'll recognize you, it's been so long."

"It's a date, see you about seven o'clock."

By nine, Jake and Ellen were falling into bed at Ellen's apartment. Jake did his best to make up for his lack of attention to Ellen, and it was after ten before they finally had satisfied themselves and nestled against each other.

"I've got a rough few days ahead," Jake said, "I had a dozen calls today from the national press so I have a ton of appointments to coordinate. But there's good news. The Florida game is going to be a big deal, nationally televised on Saturday night. Harvey suggested I bring someone along to help me. All the other girls in the department are busy, so I figure I'd ask you if you want to go."

"Gee, thanks. Don't kid around about those other girls, I hear the way they talk about you. They drool over you right in front of me. It's particularly insulting since they know we're dating."

Jake ignored the comment. He'd gotten a lot of attention from women for as long as he could remember, and had never become comfortable with it. He simply kissed Ellen long and hard, and then changed the subject.

"The game is on Saturday night, so we leave early Friday morning. The flight back is Sunday afternoon."

"That sounds like it will be fun. Really, Jake, everyone just needs to sit back and enjoy this season and not get uptight about it. People around the office are getting so worked up. There has never, ever been anything like this at Lincoln State and it may never happen again. Promise me, you'll be your usual professional self, but not act all disappointed and stuff if we lose, OK?"

"It's a deal," Jake said, "But I will be disappointed if we don't take full advantage of the rest of this night."

Chapter Eighteen

On the Tuesday following the New Mexico State game, Jake invited Harvey to lunch with the excuse of wanting to update him on the latest developments in the police investigation.

"I'm supposed to meet Sheila today at Maldaner's, downtown on Sixth Street. But why don't you tag along? We can talk in the car," Harvey suggested.

Jake wasn't crazy about not having more time with Harvey one-on-one. And from his few brief encounters with Sheila, he didn't relish the idea of getting to know her better. But with his schedule jammed for the rest of the week, Jake reluctantly agreed.

"Great," Harvey said, "come up to my office at twelve and we'll take my car downtown."

As Harvey and Jake walked to the parking lot, Harvey asked, "So, what's new with the investigation? You haven't given me any news since the police let me off the hook a couple weeks ago."

"I figured no news was good news," Jake said as he got into the passenger's seat, "but I thought you'd want to know that there has been no progress in the investigation."

Harvey grimaced, and Jake got the distinct impression that Harvey was acting more concerned than he really was. "That's unfortunate. When something like this happens on campus, everyone is on edge until it gets solved. And it would sure be nice if Jennifer's parents could get some closure. They seemed like good folks when we met them at her funeral."

"I have to tell you," Jake said, "that the police will be coming back to the athletic department. Almost all murders are committed by someone the victim knows and the detective said that he's exhausted all other aspects of her life. So they are back to thinking someone she knew in the department knows what happened. You were close to her. Do you have any ideas?"

There was a pause before Harvey answered, "I really don't, Jake. That detective has spoken with everyone in the office that she knew."

"I think he'll want to talk to some people again," Jake said.

Harvey turned onto Sixth Street and cruised slowly, looking for a parking spot near the restaurant. Maldaner's was a

Springfield landmark, open since 1884, and a traditional meeting place for many of the movers and shakers of the city. "Top-notch food," Harvey said, "but finding a place to park is a royal pain."

After finally securing a parking spot, Harvey and Jake walked two blocks to the restaurant and stepped in. Sheila had not yet arrived, so Harvey got a table for three and he and Jake sat down. The dining room had an impressively high ceiling, stunning wood floors and natural brick walls, highlighted by dark wood cabinets.

"Sheila loves this place," Harvey said, "and the food is great. Oh, here she is now."

Sheila Elwood breezed into the dining room and approached the table. "Hello, darling," she said to Harvey as she regarded Jake, "I see we have a guest joining us for lunch."

"You remember Jake Goodman," Harvey said.

"Of course, I've seen you in Harvey's office and we met at the picnic – it seems so long ago, doesn't it?"

"Nice to see you again, Mrs. Elwood," Jake said as he started to stand up from his chair.

"Please sit, Jake, although I appreciate your good manners; a rare quality in younger people today. And call me Sheila."

The difference in Sheila from the other times he bumped into her was striking. Jake always got the definite impression that Sheila was arrogant and cold, but today she was energetic and happy. She rested her hand on top of Harvey's while she continued talking to Jake, "Harvey speaks very highly of you, Jake. He tells me at least once a week what an amazing job you are doing, and under such difficult circum-stances! This has certainly been a trying few months."

"Thank you, Sheila. It's been exciting for me. I started this job at a very thrilling time. It's been keeping me busy, that's for sure."

Looking at the two of them together, it seemed to Jake that the damage to their marriage from Harvey's affair had been totally repaired, and then some. Harvey and Sheila were act-ing like newlyweds and Sheila treated Harvey with respect and affection, something noticeably absent previous times he'd seen them together.

The rest of the lunch was pleasant and cordial. Sheila talked excitedly about various charity projects she was involved with, and flashed a smile to almost every group of people entering and leaving the dining room. For many of the people she saw, she gave Harvey and Jake a quick summary of their names and how they fit into the Springfield social scene. Sheila was a walking encyclopedia on the subject of the capi-tal city's well-to-do.

Harvey said, "It was a wonderful treat seeing you in the mid-dle of the day, Sheila, but Jake and I have to get back to work." Harvey kissed Sheila on the cheek.

A wonderful treat seeing you? Jake thought as he stood up and shook Sheila's hand, narrowly avoiding a hug. It was com-mon knowledge around the athletic department office that Harvey did nothing but avoid Sheila and complained constantly about her. Jake was quiet as they started the drive back to the office, trying to mentally process what he had witnessed. Harvey interrupted his thoughts, saying, "You probably noticed that Sheila and I are getting along much better these days."

"You told me she knew about you seeing Jennifer. It looks as if she has forgiven you."

"Yes, she has. When the rumors were going around, I decided to come clean with her. It was rough for a couple of weeks and we almost split up. But to tell you the truth, this whole thing has strengthened our marriage. We're closer than we've been in twenty years. Hell, even longer than that."

Jake didn't know how to respond and simply said, "I'm happy to hear that."

***

It was after ten on Tuesday night when Slim Haskins finished for the day and left the football offices. College football coaches work back-breaking hours, especially during the season, and Slim Haskins was no exception. He arrived that morning at the usual five a.m. and put in a seventeen-hour day. In season, he typically worked seven days a week, but during the off-season he cut back to ten or twelve hour days, and only five or six days a week. He was essentially the CEO of the football team, a multi-million dollar enterprise with over a hundred employees. An assistant head coach served as the Vice President and the other assistant coaches were middle managers.

Assistants worked long schedules too, but the head coach's policy was to arrive earlier and stay later than the rest of his staff. Slim attributed his constant state of grouchiness to the long hours. But whenever he thought about his brutal schedule, he reminded himself that here were fewer than 120 head coaching jobs in Division 1-A (otherwise known as the "Football Bowl Subdivision" or FBS). As a head coach of a lower-tier FBS school, Haskins earned a little less than four hundred thousand a year, plus the chance at another hundred thousand based on team performance. Head coaches at schools in major conferences like the Big Ten and Southeast earned a million or more per season. But even for a lower-tier job like Lincoln State, if he didn't want to work the long hours there were literally thousands of others who would be happy to take his place.

As Haskins walked to his car, the now-familiar P.O.S. Oldsmobile appeared out of nowhere. The guy must park somewhere down the street and wait for me, Slim Haskins thought.

"An unexpected pleasure," Slim Haskins said, his voice dripping with sarcasm.

"Yeah. I thought about your idea of transferring the dough instead of using cash. I opened an account today at PNC Bank. That's a big bank, lots of locations all over this part of the country. Here's the account information." McGrew held out a wrinkled piece of paper.

Haskins grabbed the paper and stuffed it into his pocket. He stepped close to McGrew and made his best intimidating expression as he got right in his face, "After that transfer, it better be the last I hear from you. This is a one-shot deal, you've bled me dry."

McGrew snapped back, "It will be the end of it. There's another score I'm working on, the guy's just as big a fish as you. Then I'm blowing this shithole of a town. Just make the transfer and you'll never hear from me again." He walked away and got into his car.

***

Sheila Elwood finished her United Fund meeting at about four o'clock and headed for home. She pulled into the long horseshoe shaped brick driveway and admired her house as she approached it. It was a two-story Tudor with impressive stonework and arches, a little over five-thousand square feet, with a yard that was manicured in great detail by a part-time gardener. Her home was an impressive house by any standard and one of the finest in the Springfield area.

She thought about her lunch with Harvey and that young Goodman fellow. Just a few weeks ago, her marriage was in tatters and she was at a crossroads. How things had changed. A little forgiveness on both their parts, coupled with the threat of an expensive divorce and Harvey fell right into line. After nearly thirty years of manipulating Harvey, she knew what worked and what didn't.

Sheila could see it in their faces; so many people looked at her like she was a mere hanger-on to a successful ex-football star. Little did they know what happened behind the scenes in their relationship. Harvey was an empty headed, skirt chasing boob. When he retired from the NFL, he lacked any sort of motivation or plan for his future. In the early years of their marriage, he gave little thought to anything beyond what pretty young thing he could get into the sack. Sheila put up with his cheating and other bullshit while patiently setting a path for Harvey that led to a successful career in business and eventually becoming Athletic Director at Lincoln State. She invested the money he saved during his football career, not allowing Harvey the chance to fritter it away. He made a pittance compared to the spoiled NFL brats of today, but with smart investing on her part, it grew to a hefty sum.

If Harvey could stick with Lincoln State a few more years, they could retire in the style to which Sheila was convinced that she deserved. And she was determined that nothing would prevent that from happening.

When Harvey was named as a suspect in the murder of the girl, Sheila was livid, but not because he was cheating. What upset her is that he stupidly got the girl pregnant; a student who was his subordinate, for Christ's sake. Then the girl ended up dead. That was the sort of scandal that could end a man's career. Fortunately it worked out; the girl was gone and although there was plenty of rumor and innuendo, there was no factual evidence that she and Harvey had an affair. After her usual careful consideration, Sheila decided the best course of action was to stay with the plan, which meant staying married to the nitwit Harvey.

But at the same time, Sheila learned a valuable lesson. A friend whose opinion she greatly valued once said, "Honey works infinitely better than vinegar when it comes to keeping a man happy." Sheila decided to smother Harvey with kindness and affection, with the goal of keeping him from seeking these same things from young women. So far, it seemed to be working. For his part, Harvey also knew how close to the edge of ruining his life he had come, and was a changed man, He seemed to be soaking in the love and attention Sheila was lavishing on him like a dry sponge soaks up water.

With years of experience plotting for success, Sheila knew there were still a few major bumps in the road directly ahead. But she was fully confident she would steer the course of events to achieve her goals. No matter what it took, just like always.

***

On Saturday, the Lincoln State Abes were set to host the Tulsa Golden Hurricane. "I don't get why they have that name," Ellen said to Jake on Friday night, "there aren't hurricanes in Oklahoma."

"You got me," Jake answered, "it's Hurricane – singular – so maybe once a long time ago a stray hurricane ended up in Oklahoma, sucked up a bunch of golden wheat from the farm fields and that's how they got the name."

"Not that the Abes is a great name – in fact it's really dumb," Ellen said, "but there are plenty of silly college team names that relate to the area the school is located in. Like the Oklahoma Sooners and the Nebraska Cornhuskers. Of course, there's the Ohio State Buckeyes, the only team in college sports named after a poisonous nut."

"At least those have some meaning. What about schools that just pull a name out of thin air that's completely irrelevant? Like the Central Florida Golden Knights. As if there were ever knights running around Florida. Or the name Tigers. Are tigers roaming near Louisiana State University, or South Carolina, where Clemson is? Maybe the Abes isn't such a bad name after all."

Tulsa was having a mediocre year but turned out to be a major challenge for Lincoln State. The fans watching from the stands were split in their opinion as to whether the Abes were complacent after the lopsided victory against New Mexico State, or if they were looking past the Golden Hurricane to their huge match-up with Florida the following Saturday.

In any case, last minute heroics were required to pull out a narrow win for the third time in the season. The Abes trailed by four points, 10-6 late in the fourth quarter. The offense, which scored at will the previous week, only mustered a pair of field goals during the whole game. With the ball at their own twenty with less than ninety seconds to play, the home fans were too nervous to sit in their seats. Fans throughout the entire sold-out stadium were on their feet, hoping to avoid a shocking upset that would effectively end the Abes dream season.

This game it was the offense that came through.

Jeff Atkins was an outstanding student, a senior studying pre-med with a 3.95 GPA. Up until the previous week, he was a solid substitute tight end and recognized more for his grades (he was an academic All-American three years running) than his on-the-field accomplishments. He was called upon to be the starter a week earlier for the first time in his career when the starting tight end was suspended for the season.

In attendance that day was Jeff's widower father, who worked at the Caterpillar plant in Peoria, Illinois and attended every Lincoln State home game whether his son played much or not. On this particular day, his father was rewarded by seeing his son score a miraculous touchdown that was destined to go down in Lincoln State history.

The play started out like any other pass play. On second down, the play called for a pass over the middle to wide receiver Tavaris Adams, who was streaking across the field about fifteen yards from the line of scrimmage. As the tight end, Jeff Atkins was the safety valve on the play, a target only if no one else was open. Jeff was supposed to block at the line for a count of three, and then find an open spot in the middle about seven yards downfield.

The quarterback found Tavaris Adams open across the middle and threw a bullet pass right into the receiver's chest. Adams caught the ball and took two full steps before the safety for Tulsa hit him with a crushing helmet to the center of the chest. As Adams fell down, the ball popped six feet in the air, and the crowd gasped as two Tulsa defenders headed for it. A game-killing turnover looked almost certain.

As the ball popped up, Jeff Atkins had just started heading

for an open spot. At that instant, the Tulsa defenders leaped for the ball. The defenders collided with each other as one of them tipped the ball and kept it aloft just in time for Jeff Atkins to snare it from mid-air.

One of the factors that kept Jeff Atkins sitting on the bench most of his career was that he was not the fastest of receivers. In fact, even for a tight end he was painfully slow. But Jeff Atkins did weigh in at two-hundred-sixty pounds and once he had a head of steam, he was as hard to stop as a freight train. In one of the longest-lasting touchdown plays in Lincoln State history, Jeff Atkins eventually lumbered across the goal line with the winning score. The Abes pulled out the win 13-10.

The showdown with the undefeated and number one ranked Florida Gators loomed the following Saturday. That night as Jake fell asleep with Ellen in his arms, his main hope was that Lincoln State could get through the following week with no major crisis in the athletic department.

Chapter Nineteen

Tuesday evening at six-thirty, Slim Haskins arrived at the studios of WFMB, "Springfield's Sports Voice," for his weekly call-in show. Most head coaches supplemented their earnings from the school with side deals, and one of the most common was to appear on a weekly radio and TV show during the season. Some coaches made six figures on their various side businesses and an elite few made over a million dollars a year. As a coach lacking charisma at a lower tier school in a small market, Slim Haskins considered himself lucky to add forty or fifty thousand a year extra to his income.

Waiting to greet Slim was "Lefty" Johnson, the "Voice of the Abes" on radio broadcasts of Lincoln State games. Lefty was the moderator of the *The Don Haskins Show*; he did all the planning and kept the pace moving during the hour-long show. Slim Haskins typically showed up a half-hour before air time and Lefty provided a quick preview of what they would talk about. Once on air, Lefty lobbed softball questions to Slim, although there was also a twenty-minute segment where listeners could call in. Sometimes Slim was able to strong-arm a player to join him in the studio (unpaid of course), but this week he was alone. Slim explained to Lefty that the Atkins kid who caught the touchdown pass the week prior had the nerve to turn him down with the excuse he had to study for a test.

"Don't worry, Don, we have plenty to talk about," Left said. For some reason, he was one of the few people who didn't address Haskins as "Slim."

"What's the line-up for tonight?" Slim asked.

"Nothing out of the ordinary. We review last week's game – I'll lead you with questions, we'll take calls for a while and then preview next week's game. Like I said, we have lots to discuss. That was a great win and the Florida game will be a barn burner."

The show went as it typically did. Although he lacked a sparkling personality, Slim Haskins could talk football with the best of them. The part of the show he hated each week was the listener question segment. Slim believed that every casual football fan in Central Illinois imagined themselves as head coach of Lincoln State and in their fantasies they were all far superior coaches to Slim Haskins. Second guessing abounded among radio show callers in every city he'd ever worked in. What the coach noticed over the years of doing call-in radio was that there was no satisfying most fans. If their team lost, callers were understandably upset. But even when they won, a large group of fans loved to complain that the margin of victory wasn't enough and dwell on minor mistakes made by the Abes instead of basking in the pleasure of the win.

This season was particularly frustrating – here was Lincoln State, ranked in the top ten nationally for the first time since the playing days of Harvey Elwood. And on the phone is some farmer from Menard County who got off his tractor just long enough to call in and bitch about a missed field goal or some player's shirt not being tucked into his pants. Every week the coach the coach left the studio thinking, every guy who listens to sports talk shows and reads the sports section of the newspaper is convinced he's a football genius.

This evening's show had a typically annoying call. The caller started by saying, "I spotted something your receivers are doing on every play that tips off whether it's going to be a pass or run."

Slim Haskins sat up straight in his chair. One worry of coaches is that their players have small habits that tip-off the opposing team as to what the play will be. For instance, sometimes an offensive lineman used a slightly different stance on a running play versus a pass play, or leaned in the direction that a run was going in. Haskins and his coaches worked constantly to spot and eliminate these tendencies because they gave the opposing team a huge advantage. So if this caller saw something that he and his staff missed, it would be extremely helpful.

"Tell me more," Slim Haskins said.

"I guessed right on four out of five plays whether it was a run or pass," the caller said, "by the way your receivers acted."

"What was it they did?"

"Well, I was watching the game on TV and it wasn't any one thing...but on pass plays, the receivers always looked, you know, more interested than on running plays."

Haskins glanced at Lefty Johnson, who was rolling his eyes and trying to keep from laughing. At the same time, Johnson had worked with Haskins long enough that he kept his finger poised over the mute button on the console.

"They looked *more interested*?"

"Yeah," the caller said, "It was obvious. I can't believe you and your coaching staff missed it. I sat there with the missus, and I was right whether it was a pass or run almost every time. Well, most of the time anyway. You want me to put her on the phone? She'll tell you."

At this point, Lefty Johnson looked like he was going to fall on the floor in laughter. Unlike the host, Slim was not amused. Lefty Johnson noticed the coach looked like he was ready to blow a gasket and stepped in to disarm the situation, "I haven't noticed anything like that, and as the radio announcer for all Lincoln State football games I see every play."

"Well then, you are either blind or you don't know anything about football," the caller said.

Regaining his composure but still steaming, Slim Haskins said, "Let me tell you something, sir. Our receivers are specifically coached to stand in a certain posture, and hold their arms and hands in a certain way, on every single play – whether it is a run or pass. Believe it or not, we work on this sort of thing at almost every practice. And we look for it in the game film, which by the way, my coaches and I spend over a hundred man-hours each week reviewing."

The caller caught the deadly tone in Slim's voice and immediately tried to cover his tracks, "I didn't mean anything...you know, I was just, you know...trying to help."

"Yeah, well, I will certainly tell our receivers coach to instruct his guys to be less interested on pass plays and more interested on running plays in the Florida game."

Lefty pushed the disconnect button to end the call and quickly called for a commercial break.

Slim Haskins let out a long, hissing sigh. Such was the life of a college football coach, even the coach of a top-ten ranked team.

***

The bank notified Ken McGrew Tuesday morning that his new account was now a hundred thousand dollars richer. Receiving the deposit was the ex-cop's go-ahead to start the second phase of his plan. He got in his Oldsmobile and headed for the athletic office parking lot. As he made the fifteen-minute drive, he daydreamed about which model car he would buy with a fraction of his new-found wealth. A BMW

wasn't out of the question, he thought, because he anticipated receiving another hundred grand within the next few
days. Not one of the big ones; he'd go for one of the smaller,
sporty models.

It was an hour before lunch, and the parking lot at a campus
burger joint across from the athletic building was still wide
open. McGrew pulled into it and made sure he could see the
comings and goings of athletic department staff. A few minutes past eleven, Slim Haskins ducked out of the door,
looked around and walked across the street to McGrew's
car. McGrew dropped the small recorder into the coach's
outstretched hand and Haskins stomped off without a word.
"Nice doing business with you!" McGrew called out.

Ken McGrew didn't leave, but settled into the well-worn
seat and waited. Shortly after noon, he saw Harvey Elwood
come out the door alone and drive off in his SUV. Ken
McGrew eased behind Harvey's vehicle, keeping several car
lengths between them. Harvey had retained his services a
few times and knew McGrew by sight, but it was highly
unlikely that Harvey would think twice about the beat-up
Oldsmobile that was following him.

Harvey pulled into the Hilton hotel parking lot and walked
into the attached Bennigan's restaurant. McGrew parked in
a corner spot of the same lot, pulled out the latest copy of the
newspaper and got comfortable in the front seat of the
Oldsmobile. A few minutes before one o'clock, McGrew got
out of his car and leaned against it in a position where he
could watch the restaurant door. About ten minutes later,
there was Harvey Elwood coming out of the restaurant with

some guy in a suit. The two men shook hands and parted company, the suit heading toward the other end of the parking lot while Harvey ambled toward his car. McGrew caught up to Harvey just as he was reaching for his car door.

"Hello, Harvey," McGrew said.

It took Harvey a few beats to pull McGrew's face from his memory. "Ken McGrew, isn't it? You're a private investigator."

"Bingo," McGrew answered, "And I have a very important matter to discuss with you."

Like everyone else who met Ken McGrew, Harvey preferred to keep personal contact to a minimum. His first thought was to brush him off, but McGrew's previous assignments from Harvey were not run through the department budget, Harvey paid McGrew cash. So Harvey figured that a downtown parking lot was preferable to meeting in the athletic office. Harvey put on a jovial face and asked, "What's on your mind?"

"I was thinking about these, and how much they're worth to you," McGrew said as he handed Harvey three photos. Harvey recognized them instantly as the ones Slim Haskins took of Harvey and Jennifer frolicking in the boathouse.

Harvey gasped, "Where did these come from? These aren't yours!"

"I acquired them from the photographer in exchange for certain favors on my part. The photos are now my property, unless you're willing to buy them from me."

He was being shaken down, Harvey thought. Although he would have liked to grab the detective by his throat, he quickly decided that the best approach was to play it very cool. "You know, I was officially cleared of Jennifer Stewart's murder. The police know we were seeing each other. So I don't know why you think I'd pay a dime for these."

"Even if the police know," McGrew said, "I never saw anything on the news saying that the two of you were doing the dirty deed. These photos would make a great story, especially with all the attention Lincoln State is getting right now. How do you think the Board of Trustees will feel about the university's middle-aged Athletic Director having a good time with his young graduate assistant and pictures of them having sex turning up on the Internet?"

Good point, Harvey thought. After he was cleared as a suspect, several members of the board called and asked about the rumors floating around regarding him and Jennifer. He denied everything vehemently and the board members backed off, but they all warned Harvey that if evidence of the affair surfaced, his job would be in great jeopardy. If these photos became public, it was almost a sure bet that he would be fired.

"Get to the point," Harvey said, "What is it that you want?"

"Simple. A hundred grand deposited in this account," McGrew handed Harvey a tattered slip of paper, "Make it by Friday of this week."

"This is ridiculous," Harvey said, "You obviously have the files for these pictures. If I give you a hundred thousand, you'll piss it away and next month you'll be back for more."

"You'll have to take my word for it. The truth is I plan to leave town; these goddamned winters are getting tiresome. Plus, you'll have a record of the wire transfer. If I double-cross you and make the photos public, you won't have anything to lose by ratting me out. You'll show the cops the paperwork and I spend a year in the slammer for extortion. So we have each other over the proverbial barrel."

It made sense to Harvey. But Sheila was going to be infuriated, to put it mildly. She went volcanic when he confided in her about the photos a couple of weeks earlier, and she wasn't going to like the fact they had resurfaced. "OK, it's a deal. I'll get you the cash."

"Smart decision," McGrew said, and walked away.

As Harvey predicted, the discussion with Sheila that evening about McGrew's demand was an unpleasant one. The term "moron" was used more times than Harvey could keep track of. Sheila hated the idea of paying McGrew but finally agreed to sleep on it.

***

Now that he had paid off that asshole blackmailer, Slim Haskins felt like a gigantic weight had been lifted from him. And just in time, he thought. The game plan for the Florida contest would take every bit of energy and time he had. It was a good thing he was unencumbered by a wife or family, because he planned on sleeping at the football offices all this week. This game was the opportunity of a lifetime, his moment to shine, and he planned on doing everything he possibly could to take advantage of it. If the Abes won this game, he wouldn't have to worry about keeping his job at Lincoln State, and he could even generate interest from bigger universities for head coaching job openings that came up. That meant there could be million-dollar paydays ahead.

Slim Haskins wasn't the only person in the athletic department working long hours that week. The Florida-Lincoln State matchup was being promoted on television as this week's "game of the year." In the past two weeks, the Abes leapfrogged over several teams. They were now ranked sixth in the nation and Florida was an undefeated number two. With several "quality wins" and their only loss coming to the Michigan State Spartans, who also had only one defeat, the Abes made it impossible for the football pollsters to keep them out of the top ten.

Jake was in meetings or on the phone from morning until night the entire week preceding the Florida game. It seemed like every major newspaper, magazine and broadcast outlet was running stories about Lincoln State. The Abes were being called the Cinderella team of the decade. Once again, Ellen had been moved to the back burner of his schedule. She understood the demands on his time and wasn't upset about it, especially since she'd be flying to Gainesville on Friday morning along with Jake.

***

An air of excitement filled the gloomy pre-dawn Friday morning as the football team and department administrators boarded the large charter jet for Gainesville. Jake settled into his seat next to Ellen and pulled the interview schedule from his briefcase.

"We'll have to hit the ground running," he warned Ellen, "Haskins, Harvey and four players are scheduled for ESPN interviews before team practice this afternoon."

"We're all set, Jake," Ellen assured him, "Everybody knows what their time slot is and where they need to be. It's under control. Don't forget to turn your phone off, it looks like they're closing the cabin door."

Jake pulled out his phone. In the rush to get on the plane, he had ignored a call from Johnny Rose and let it go to voice-mail. He dialed voicemail and listened to Johnny saying, "Jake, you won't believe this! Remember that dirt ball private eye we met last week? He was found dead in his bed early this morning. I just got a call from Eddie. He said there's no question that it was murder. Remember, that guy was in charge of security in the building where Jennifer was killed. Man, if I was in the life insurance business, I wouldn't sell a policy to someone living in that building; it's a dangerous place. My flight doesn't leave for a couple hours, plus I have a connection since I don't get to fly charter like the important people. Anyway, I'll give you a call when I get into Gaines-ville tonight."

Chapter Twenty

Jake finished his work duties around 7 o'clock and found Ellen waiting in the hotel room. "How about some room service?" she asked.

"Sounds great. I don't feel much like going out, for now anyway. I'm sure Johnny will want to get a drink later when he gets into town."

As they waited for their food, Ellen asked about the afternoon interviews. Jake answered, "Everything went perfect. I can't get over the media frenzy about this game. It really has fans excited."

"Well, there's a lot at stake," Ellen said, "If we win, Florida probably drops out of the top ten, or at least the top five. And we would go to a major bowl game."

"But there seems to be more to it than just that, this time of year there's a game every week that's important to the rankings," Jake answered, "There's a David-and-Goliath factor that has captured everyone's imagination. Powerful programs like the Florida usually only play teams like Lincoln State because they're an easy win, so this is a very special situation."

"Yeah, I read about how hard it is for small schools that have gotten a reputation for being hard to beat, like Boise State and Texas Christian, to get games against teams like Florida. If you're not a pushover, national powers avoid playing you like the plague."

"True," Jake said, "but it's easy to see why. If Florida wins tomorrow, everyone will say they should have beaten tiny Lincoln State, no big deal. But if they lose their fans will treat it like the end of the world."

"Yeah, it's a no-win situation for the power schools."

Jake said, "When the schedule was set three years ago, Lincoln State looked like the next best thing to a week off. I'm sure this game is a very unwelcome surprise to Florida's Athletic Director. He could never have predicted that we'd be nationally ranked."

A knock on the door and the arrival of room service interrupted their discussion. After they were done eating, Jake looked at his watch. "It's after nine and still no Johnny. Maybe he decided to crash early tonight."

Ellen laughed, "I suppose there's a first time for everything."

"We may as well use this time the best way possible," Jake said as he pulled Ellen to the bed.

As usual, Jake was amazed at their lovemaking. They never had bad sex, or even average sex. It was always fantastic, incredible, memorable sex. They were still engaged, although Jake had just finished, when his phone rang loudly. He pulled out of Ellen quickly and rolled over to grab it.

"What was that about?" Ellen said, "If I was a chain saw, you would have started me!"

Jake ignored her and answered. Johnny said, "Hey buddy. What a nightmare, I'm sitting in the Atlanta airport with my thumb up my ass. My flight's delayed. Looks like I'll be getting in after midnight, so I'm just going to crash when I finally get there. What are things like in Gainesville?"

"You'll love it, the atmosphere is incredible. People are really, really pumped up about this game."

"I can't wait to get there. Christ, I'm excited about this game too. Where're you at right now?"

"Ellen and I are just hanging out in the hotel room."

"Hey, you sound out of breath, brother. You been doing pushups? Hope I interrupted something!" Jake heard laughter as Johnny hung up.

***

The nationally televised game didn't start until seven-thirty so Jake slept late the next morning. He had a couple of short interviews lined up for some of the coaches early in the day, but Jake himself had several meetings scheduled with the television and radio people. Because Lincoln State rose so unexpectedly to national prominence, the top-line broadcasters who were announcing this game knew very little about the Abes. It was important that Jake make certain the on-air people were familiar with the school so that they presented Lincoln State in the most positive light. A high profile national game like this was a huge opportunity to boost not only recruiting for Lincoln State football, but for academics as well. It was common for small schools that found themselves in an important nationally televised game to see a surge in admissions applications for several months after.

As Jake made the three-quarter mile walk from the Hilton Hotel to the stadium, he thought about the research he'd done about Ben Hill Griffin Stadium, the home of the Florida Gators. It was a notoriously difficult place to play. Florida fans referred to their stadium as "The Swamp," and the name aptly described the place as far as visiting teams were concerned. Since 1990, Florida had won nearly ninety-percent of games played on their home field.

Like many college stadiums, Ben Hill Griffin Stadium was built decades ago but the original 1930s stadium had been renovated many times and now held over 90,000 screaming fans. Interestingly, Ben Hill Griffin (who was famous in his own right as one of the wealthiest men in the U.S.) was best known in recent years as the grandfather of Katherine Harris, the Florida Secretary of State who presided over the Bush-Gore election recount fiasco.

The atmosphere around the stadium grew more and more electric through the day. By game time the stands were packed beyond capacity with rabid fans, about ninety-nine percent dressed in the blue and orange colors of the home team.

Both teams were tentative in the early going. Lincoln State's defense was strong as usual, but the Abes' offense was stagnant, so the first quarter ended with no score. The first play of the second quarter was a punt by Lincoln State, which the Florida returner caught at his own thirty yard line. He found an opening and rocketed downfield for the first touchdown of the game.

Finally, late in the second quarter, the Abes put three points on the scoreboard with a field goal to make the score 7-3. On the ensuing kickoff, the Abes got their first break of the game when Florida fumbled and Lincoln State recovered. With great field position but only thirty seconds left in the half, the Abes tried and failed on three straight passes to the end zone; they settled for another field goal to pull within a single point at halftime.

"We got them right where we want them," Slim Haskins told his players at halftime, "They're on their home turf and all they've been able to get is one touchdown on a punt return. I'll bet they're over in their locker room shitting bricks right now. The door to victory is open for us, guys. All we have to do is walk through it. Now get out there and score some points!"

The Lincoln State offense finally came alive in the second

half. The Abes took the kickoff and drove the length of the field to score a touchdown and take the lead 13-7. Inspired, the defense forced a fumble by Florida's offense a few minutes later. Onolulo Kahona, the massive Samoan defensive end, slammed into the Florida quarterback and dislodged the ball. As the ball bounced free, another Lincoln State lineman picked it up and ran into the end zone for a touchdown.

Now leading the number two team in the nation by 20-7 in the third quarter, Lincoln State tried running the ball on several plays to use up the game clock faster. It turned out to be a mistake as the Gators stopped the Abes easily, forced them to punt, and took the ball down the field two straight times for touchdowns. By the end of the third quarter, the Abes trailed 21-20 and The Swamp was going wild with cheering, jeering Florida fans. Albert Gator, the chubby, cartoonish alligator mascot for the Gators, was romping on the sidelines in front of the small Lincoln State fan area, and 90,000 Florida fans were directing their mocking "gator clap" at the tiny group of Abes fans.

The score remained the same until the middle of the final quarter. Once again, Onolulo Kahona and the Lincoln State defense forced a Florida fumble deep in Gator territory. The Abes quarterback completed two straight passes, the second one for the go-ahead touchdown with only seven minutes left in the game.

With the score at 26-21, Slim Haskins made a decisive play call. All week, the extra point squad practiced a fake where, instead of kicking the ball for one point, the holder passed it to a receiver for a two-point conversion. The play caught

Florida by surprise and Lincoln State now led 28-21. That meant Florida would have to score a touchdown and extra point just to tie the game.

The Gators fell flat on their ensuing possession, but once again Slim Haskins coached conservatively and called for three straight running plays instead of attempting a pass. Now the Gators had the ball at their own thirty-five yard line with just under three minutes left for what was probably their last chance to tie the game.

For Lincoln State fans, the next three minutes seemed like an eternity. The Gators moved the ball with ease all the way to the Lincoln State ten-yard line. Then the Abes defense stiffened and stopped the Gators for no gain on three straight plays. That made it fourth down with thirty seconds left in the contest. The entire game – the entire season – was coming down to one play. Florida's quarterback dropped back and lofted a pass toward an open receiver in the corner of the end zone. For an endless instant the ball hung in the air, and with it the fate of the Abes dream season. The Florida receiver stretched mightily for the pass but the ball was a few inches beyond his waiting hands.

A groan came from 90,000 Florida fans, followed by a shocked quiet. Lincoln State was the team on the schedule that many Florida fans complained about as being too easy for the mighty Gators, and many Florida fans sold their tickets to this game for pennies on the dollar before the season even started.

Lincoln State's offense ran out the clock with one play and

the game was over. The only cheers in the stadium came from the tiny Lincoln State contingent, about two-hundred strong.

The Hilton Hotel just off campus rocked until 4 a.m. that night. The coaches lifted the curfew with the stipulation the players remain in the spacious hotel and conference center. Even in their revelry, administration members kept a close eye on all doors to prevent players from sneaking out. Fortunately, the hotel's management had experience with visiting sports teams so they opened a large meeting room and made drinks and snacks available for the impromptu party.

The charter flight for the team, coaches and administrators didn't leave until Sunday afternoon, so everyone could relax and enjoy the monumental victory. It was a night no one would ever forget. The next day would also be memorable, for not-so-pleasant reasons.

Chapter Twenty-One

As they boarded the large charter jet, Jake said to Ellen, "Why don't we grab some seats way in the back? We can have some privacy and maybe catch a nap. I'm partied out."

"Sounds good to me," Ellen answered. They walked to the rear of the plane and snagged an entire vacant row for the two-hour flight. The nearest other passengers were three rows ahead.

The celebration continued full-steam on the return flight to Springfield. Besides the tremendous upset of the Gators, two other top five teams fell on Saturday. If they could win the following week against Iowa State at home, the Lincoln State Abes were almost certain to be invited to a major bowl game for the first time in school history. It was even possible, with the right combination of losses by certain teams, that the Abes could make it to the championship game.

As the plane landed, a tired but still elated Jake turned on his cell phone and waited for the typical emails and perhaps a routine phone message or two to show up on his display. He noticed a missed call from Eddie Martin and dialed voicemail. Just as the plane docked at the gate, Ellen watched Jake's face turn white as he listened to the message.

"What is it?" Ellen asked.

All Jake said was, "I have to get up front and talk to Harvey before anyone gets off the plane!" But the aisle was jammed with passengers and the door was already opening. Jake tried pushing his way through the aisle but found that 300-pound linemen move slowly and at their own pace.

Slim Haskins walked in the tunnel from the plane toward the gate area wondering about how many Lincoln State fans would be waiting to welcome the team home. He was still daydreaming about his hero's welcome when four police officers converged on him, with Detective Eddie Martin right behind.

Slim heard Eddie say, "Donald Haskins, you're under arrest for the murders of Jennifer Stewart and Ken McGrew..." just as the cuffs were snapped onto his wrists. As the officers quickly escorted Haskins out of the gate area and into the main terminal, Eddie walked alongside and continued reciting the Miranda rights.

The waiting crowd of about two hundred fans started to cheer as the victorious coach appeared around the corner, then when someone noticed the handcuffs , there was a confused murmur. Just as quickly, the crowd lost interest in the mystery of the coach's police escort and turned their full attention to the players and assistant coaches appeared twenty feet behind the group of police. The players were walking far enough behind the coaching staff and enjoying the adulation of the crowd too much to notice that the police were placing their coach into a waiting squad car just outside the terminal doors.

"Harvey!" Jake called out ahead. But Harvey was busy working the crowd, shaking hands and smiling broadly. Then Jake saw Johnny Rose, standing alongside a *State Journal-Register* photographer.

"Eddie gave me a little bit of a heads up," Johnny said, "he didn't tell me why but said I should be at the airport when your flight got in and to bring a photographer with me. What a shocker about Slim Haskins getting arrested, huh?"

"I don't get it," Jake said, "He had minimal contact with Jennifer. And who knows what his connection was to that sleazy private eye."

"It's weird. Anyway, Eddie said he's holding a press conference at six o'clock today. He told me he wasn't giving anyone any information until then."

***

The press conference started at six but the small media room was filled to overflowing a half-hour before. Almost every media outlet in the Midwest had rushed to get there, as well as ESPN, Fox Sports and CNN. The head football coach arrested for murder (of a co-ed no less) within twenty-four hours of one of the biggest upsets in college football history was too titillating of a story to ignore.

After the camera people were allowed into the media room, there was only enough room for a handful of reporters. Eddie made sure that Jake and Johnny were in the media room, but dozens of reporters were led to a makeshift area that was set up in the squad room. A closed-circuit television sat in front of the squad meeting room, which had about thirty school-type desks, most of which barely contained the reporters who sat in them.

Eddie walked to the front of the media room, accompanied by the police chief.

"Ladies and gentlemen, over the weekend certain evidence was found that linked Donald Haskins to the killings of Jennifer Stewart and Ken McGrew," Eddie said, "The main items of evidence were as follows: An audio recording file was found on Ken McGrew's computer of Donald Haskins having what was clearly a physical altercation with Jennifer Stewart. We believe it was this altercation that resulted in Ms. Stewart's death. Also, a surveillance photo of Mr. Haskins car in front of Ms. Stewart's residence with a date stamp of the night of the killing was found in Ken McGrew's apartment. As far as motive, we think McGrew was blackmailing Donald Haskins with the recording and photo. There was a substantial transfer of funds from Donald Haskins to Ken McGrew made last week. We think that McGrew approached Haskins for more money Thursday evening, at which time Donald Haskins killed McGrew."

After Eddie's statement, there were several questions from reporters. The sports people focused on the possibility of bail and speculated whether Slim Haskins would be available to coach. Even if Slim Haskins was released on bail he would certainly be suspended from his coaching job, if not fired, Jake thought to himself. He made a mental note to talk to Harvey first thing after the press conference. For all Jake knew, the Athletic Board could be convening at this moment to decide the fate of the coach.

Johnny and Jake sat together after the press conference, passing the time until the throng of reporters surrounding Eddie subsided.

"Do you think he did it?" Johnny asked Jake.

"There seems to be a lot of evidence. I didn't know Slim Haskins well enough to say if he had murder in him. I'm not sure anyone knows him – he's a hard guy to get to know and even harder to like. But my impression was that he was more of a hothead than a cold-blooded killer."

"I agree with you, he seemed to be more bluster and bullshit than anything else. But who really knows? And like you said, there is some strong evidence."

Jake paused. Something had just come back to him. He said, "It seemed weird to me, I heard Haskins and Jennifer arguing once. They were under the stadium near the entrance to the football offices. I didn't think much of it at the time."

"Wow, Jake. You need to mention that to Eddie. It could be important."

"I will. But right now I need to call Harvey," Jake dialed his phone, "Harvey...it's Jake here. The press conference just ended. Is there any word on what action the board is going to take or when?"

Jake gave Johnny a thumbs-down as he listened to Harvey, then he said into the phone, "OK, I'll let the press know. Maybe it'll take some of the heat off you and the board. They're all here anyway and now that they're done with Eddie I see a few of them coming this way."

Jake turned to Johnny, "The board held a conference call while they watched Eddie's press conference on television. Haskins is terminated. Joe Schuller has been named interim head coach for the rest of the season."

"Smart idea, Schuller is already the Assistant Head Coach. Some people say he's the brains behind the team anyway. He'll do all right."

At that moment, the first of several reporters stepped up to Jake. In what was basically an impromptu press conference, Jake announced the news about Slim Haskins being fired.

Early the next morning, Jake walked by Harvey's office and noticed the Athletic Director was already in.

"Getting an early start today?" Jake asked.

"Just like you, I'm being bombarded with phone calls and emails. Everyone wants a comment on the situation."

"Can you give me some details on the board's decision in case I'm asked about it?"

"I organized a conference call and we all watched the press conference on TV. It was a slam dunk once they announced Haskins was being charged with murder."

It seemed to Jake that Harvey was quite happy that Slim Haskins was in jail. "So what would happen if he's cleared of the charges?"

"First, I don't see that happening. I think he did it. Second, he is finished at Lincoln State. Make that clear to everyone. Stick a fork in Slim Haskins because he's done. Set up a meet-the-press thing for Joe Schuller this afternoon. Let me know what time, I want to be there too."

Just then Harvey's phone rang. It was the Springfield police. Harvey listened for a minute, then said emphatically, "Tell him no fucking way. Use those words. He does not have the support of the university in any way, shape or form."

Harvey hung up the phone and said to Jake, "That was the police. Haskins requested me to come down to the jail and meet with him to discuss getting him out of the slammer."

"It might be a good P.R. move to support him, at least until he's proven guilty or innocent."

"Absolutely not. That asshole is on his own. To tell you the truth, I've been looking forward to this day."

"I've got to get started on setting up the meeting with Coach Schuller. I'll let you know the details." Jake got up and left Harvey's office.

The introduction of Joe Schuller as temporary head coach

went smoothly. It was helpful that Schuller had a more engaging personality than Slim Haskins and he seemed completely at ease in dealing with the media. Jake hoped the new coach was as good at getting the Abes ready for the game on Saturday against Iowa State as he was at talking.

***

The next morning, Jake was back in his typical routine of game preparation when the phone rang. He was shocked to hear Slim Haskins on the phone.

"Jake, this is Don Haskins. Don't hang up on me, OK?"

"What is it? Where are you calling from?"

"Don't worry, I'm still in jail. There isn't a mad killer loose on the streets. I got them to let me call you. Listen, I'm desperate. You gotta help me. Everyone at the university has turned their back on me. I've tried Harvey, Milt, everyone I know on the board. They all think I'm guilty and are hanging me out to dry."

Jake didn't know how to respond so he just said, "Why are you calling me?"

"You're my last hope. I know you think I'm a prick. But I didn't kill that girl or the detective. I'm being set up."

"Who would set you up and why?"

"I don't have the slightest idea. But I'm innocent. And no one believes me. I even got a lawyer, one of those three-hundred-buck-an-hour guys. He looked at me like I was a bug on the windshield of his Mercedes. Like he knew I was guilty and didn't care one way or another what happened to me."

"What do you think I can do for you?"

"Figure out who killed those people! I know you were looking into the girl's killing and you're friends with that detective who arrested me. You've got connections around the city, people who might know something. Help me, please! You're my last hope."

Jake sighed. How did he end up in the middle of this? "I'll talk to Detective Martin. That's all I can promise. We'll see what happens from there."

"I guess that's all I can ask for. Just let me know one way or another, OK? "

"All right. I'll talk to the detective and be in touch in the next day or two."

***

"I think he's telling the truth," Jake said to Eddie, slapping the restaurant table.

"Christ almighty, Jake. Look at the evidence. We have audio of Haskins and Jennifer having an argument. You can actually hear him hit her. Then, you hear Haskins apparently cleaning up the place before he left. The District Attorney is going for murder two on the girl because it sounds on the recording like he just popped her one in anger, then panicked and hit her with a statue to finish her off. The D.A wants first degree murder for McGrew because of the blackmail motive."

"But the guy says he didn't do it."

Johnny Rose piped in, "Jake, the state prison up in Joliet is full of innocent men. There's not one guilty person in there. Just ask them, they'll tell you."

"Then let's do this," Jake said, "Why don't we talk to Haskins? Johnny, maybe he'll give you something for a story."

Eddie said, "Here's what we'll do. I'll give you access to Haskins for a half-hour. I won't be in the interview room; it'll just be you three. But your end of the deal is to tell me every single word Haskins says. I want to question him later and I'll see if his story matches the one he tells you."

***

The interview room was cold and stark, about eight-by-ten feet with cinderblock walls and a worn linoleum floor. A six-foot metal table was bolted to the floor in the center of the room. On one side of the table was a stainless steel bench, also bolted to the floor, and on the other side were two plastic-bucket chairs. Eddie led Johnny and Jake into the room, gestured to the chairs and left the room. The thick metal door closed loudly. There was a video camera mounted in one corner of the room, but Eddie told them it would be illegal to record their session so the camera was turned off.

A uniformed officer led a handcuffed Slim Haskins in and sat him on the steel bench.

Haskins smiled sadly and said, "This is a far cry from where I was a few days ago, huh? I had the world by the balls on Sunday, and now I'm in a world of shit."

"Sometimes you're the pigeon and sometimes you're the statue," Jake joked lamely, and immediately wished he hadn't said it.

Johnny said, "We talked to the detective, coach, and the evidence against you is really strong. If you want us to help you, then you need to convince us you're innocent. Tell us your side of things."

"Let's start with the girl. I did something very stupid. Remember the welcome picnic? Goodman, you met me there. I saw Harvey Elwood and Jennifer Stewart sneak off. They were looking over their shoulders heading for the boathouse. I thought, 'what the fuck?' and followed them. It turns out they were having some kissy-kissy time and a whole lot more. I climbed up on a boat and started snapping pictures through the window with my phone camera. I got lucky – there were a couple of very incriminating shots, if you know what I mean. Remember before the season started? Everybody and their brother was calling for my head. I figured those photos were job security, so I showed them to the girl."

"Is that what I heard you arguing with her about under the stands by the football offices?"

"Yeah, we argued every time we talked, which I think was on three occasions. She was very pissed off. Anyway, she was supposed to get Harvey to renew my contract and she was stalling. So I got her address from employee records and dropped in to see her that night she was killed. We argued and she took a swing at me. I pushed her and she fell against the fireplace. But she was OK when I left."

"Was she standing?"

"No, she was groggy, semi-conscious. I realize that sounds bad but I've seen my share of head injuries and she was starting to come around. She was going to be all right."

"Did you know about the recording?"

"That sleazy investigator was blackmailing me with the recording and the photo of my car in front of the girl's building. He gave me a voice recorder, in fact, it's in my office desk. I didn't know he had a file on his PC, the stupid idiot didn't bother to delete it. You know, he said something interesting the last time I talked to him. He said that he had another score in the works and it would pay off soon. Then he was going to leave town."

"Did he say anything about what this second score was?"

"No. I talked to him as little as possible."

"Did you happen to be at McGrew's apartment that night, just like you happened to be at Jennifer's the same night she was killed?"

"No, I wasn't there. But I don't have an alibi, I was working alone as usual."

"I don't have any more questions," Johnny said, "how about you, Jake?"

Jake turned to Slim Haskins and looked him in the eye, "If

you didn't kill the two of them, then who do you think did it?"

"I have no fucking idea. That's why I need your help. The cops already have me pegged as guilty; they won't look at anybody else. And the athletic department has already written me off. Like I told you on the phone, Goodman, you're my last chance."

Chapter Twenty-Two

After Slim Haskins was led out of the interview room, Eddie Martin walked in and sat on the steel bench.

"So, amateur crime fighters, what did you find out?"

Jake relayed the story exactly as Slim Haskins told it. Johnny said to Eddie, "I'm not a fan of Slim Haskins, but I believe him. How 'bout you let us hear the recording, Eddie?"

"I'll let you hear it, but off the record as far as you're concerned, John. I don't want to read a transcript in the *Journal-Register*."

"No problem, let's do it."

In his office, Eddie played the audio on his PC speakers, and said, "You understand now? Haskins killed her. He pushed her into the fireplace, hit her a couple times with the nearest blunt object and then cleaned up after himself while she was dying."

"That's open to interpretation," Jake said, "Play it again."

A few seconds after the part where Haskins pushed Jennifer, Jake cried, "Stop here! Did you hear him? He mumbled, 'Oh Christ.' Where does he hit her again?"

"Right here," Eddie said, and hit play again. There were two distinct clunking sounds.

"Those could be anything," Jake said, "they weren't that loud."

"They sound a lot like him smacking the victim with a blunt object," Eddie said.

They listened again to the rest of the recording, and just heard rustling around Jennifer's apartment for about three minutes followed by a quiet opening and closing of the door.

"How long does the recording last?" Jake said.

"It's quiet for about three more minutes, after which the original recorder must have gotten full or was shut off."

"Who recorded this? Was McGrew using some bugging device?"

Eddie said, "No, this was a pocket recorder that Harvey Elwood said he gave the victim for a 'special project' they were working on. That's complete bullshit, but in any event she had the recorder on her the night she was killed. Haskins said that McGrew gave it to him in exchange for a hundred grand, which is another mystery – how did McGrew end up with it? Haskins said he was sure he put it in his desk in his office at the stadium. We searched everywhere, there and his home. No luck, it's not anywhere. Which also makes you wonder about his story. My theory is that Haskins hit the girl and then panicked and killed her. Then he got black-mailed by McGrew and killed him as well.

That, by the way, is also the belief of the Chief of Police, the President of Lincoln State, the Mayor, the Athletic Director and the head of the Board of Trustees. A whole bunch of im-portant people with the same theory means a lot of pressure on me. If I start chasing other leads when we have a suspect sitting in jail, I guarantee you that my ass will be in the chief's office getting chewed out. The powers-that-be want this cased wrapped up and tied with a bow. Unless I have something stronger than your interpretation of the recording and the word of Slim Haskins, then this case is closed as far as I'm concerned."

As Jake started his car in the police department parking lot, he said to Johnny, "I've just got this hunch, I can't explain why. But I'm not convinced that Slim Haskins did it."

"I'm with you, buddy. It all seems too neat and tidy to me. I don't blame Eddie. But there are a lot of holes in his theory, particularly how McGrew got in the middle of all this and what part he played. If you want, let's put our heads together and see what else we can find out."

"I'm on board with that. But let me get the next few days behind me. The Iowa State game is this Saturday."

***

The Lincoln State football team responded to their new coach and defeated the Iowa State Cyclones 21-10 to finish the regular season with ten wins and only one loss. As usual, Jake coordinated the after-game interviews and press conferences. Everyone – from Harvey to most reporters to the coaching staff – acted like Slim Haskins was a distant memory. A few players mentioned the former coach's name, but other than that, it came up only once in a question by a reporter which was answered with a terse reply. The other reporters took the hint and stayed away from the topic.

Jake, Ellen and Johnny went out for dinner Saturday evening and Ellen commented on how quickly Slim Haskins had become an afterthought.

Johnny answered, "It's because of two things. Foremost, everyone is focused on the fact that Lincoln State is going to a major bowl game for the first time in history. But I've noticed something else in the past few days. My big boss – the Editor in Chief – dropped by to see me on Thursday. He told me that it was in the best interest of everyone if I didn't mention Slim Haskins in any stories and focused on the positive aspects of the football program. My guess is that someone with a lot of juice talked to him and strongly suggested that idea."

"What do you mean, focus on the positive?" Jake asked. That wasn't coming from Sports Information – I knew nothing about it."

"Someone from above went around you on this one, Jake. For some reason, they want Slim Haskins to fade away and rot in jail. Like I said before, the guy is an asshole and I never liked him. Now he's possibly a murderer. But it strikes me as odd that somebody wants him forgotten as quickly as possible."

Jake said, "It makes me even more curious about these murders. I really think we should look into this, Johnny."

"Can we please talk about something else?" Ellen pleaded, "We should be celebrating and you two are making it all doom and gloom with your conspiracy theories."

"You're right," Jake said, "The big bowl invitations come out next week. Where do you think we're going?"

The three spent the rest of the evening debating which bowl would select the Abes and the merits of the various sunny locations where they might be spending New Year's Day.

***

The following week was hectic as the university prepared for the bowl fever that was sure to infect the school and the surrounding area. Johnny and Jake were equally absorbed in their jobs all week, but agreed to get together on Thursday evening for dinner.

Jake walked into Augie's Front Burner and saw Johnny sitting at the bar.

"Kind of an upscale place for us, isn't this?" Jake asked.

"Yeah, but it's good food, man. I was downtown for a meeting and I thought I might introduce some class into your life."

They asked for a quiet table. "People are going to start getting the wrong idea about our get-togethers," Jake said, "I should have had Ellen come with me."

Johnny said, "Naw, it's better with just us guys. I wanted to ask you, what's your guess on what bowl game we're going to?"

"I think we'll be going to Arizona," Jake said.

"We should be going to the title game," Johnny said, "but I don't think that'll happen. We're ten-and-one. There are no undefeated teams, but there are six other teams with only one loss. It's a very long shot we'll be ranked in the top two."

"Well, the talk in the athletic office this week has been about how a bowl game is a two-sided coin. It's great because the football team gets three extra weeks of practice – that doesn't seem like much but it really makes a difference. Players develop much faster, especially the freshmen and sophomores. Plus a big bowl game is an amazing recruiting tool, especially for a small school like us. We get national TV exposure for a month and just about every football fan in the country will be watching the game, no matter where we end up."

"It's a sweet deal, but the financial risk is the downside."

"Exactly right. The big bowl games are big money. But few people realize that Lincoln State will have to buy a huge block of tickets in advance. If we sell them all, great. But if we don't, we could lose our ass. Back in 2009, Ohio State went to the Fiesta Bowl – and they had to buy 17,500 tickets in advance. They sold fewer than 10,000 tickets and they lost over a million dollars on the bowl."

"Actually their conference lost the money. All their teams throw their bowl earnings and expenses into a big pot and then the whole conference splits what's left over when the dust settles."

"But we aren't splitting the money or the risk with anyone because Lincoln State isn't in a BCS conference. We'll live or die with how many tickets we sell. In 2008, Western Michigan went to the Texas Bowl and had to pay $450,000 for 11,000 tickets. They sold 548 tickets and lost over four hundred grand."

"I don't think we have to worry. People are already falling all over themselves to line up for tickets and they don't even know where we're going yet. But the bowl system is weird. And it's mind-boggling how much money some of those bowl games make."

Jake said, "A major bowl like we're going to may take in $20 million or more in revenue. They pay out maybe half of that to the teams involved. That leaves $10 million just for managing one college football game that lasts maybe four hours. Some of the administrators in charge of the big bowls get paid a half-million bucks a year."

"Some bowls make charitable donations. But not as much as many people think. In 2009, all the bowls in total donated just over three million dollars to charity, less than two percent of their revenues."

"But you know what? We're happy to go. The benefits out-weigh the negatives. It's almost unheard of for a school to turn down a bowl invitation, and certainly not from a major bowl. Our fans live for this."

Johnny said, "OK, enough sports talk. My schedule will open up in a couple of days, once the bowl announcement blows over. And you'll have a little free time on your hands for a change. Do you still want to help Haskins and check things out?"

"I've been thinking about it," Jake said, "and we need to. I can't shake this feeling that there's more to all that's been happening than just Slim Haskins."

"I'm with you. But I talked to Eddie and he says as far as he's concerned the case is solved, so we're on our own. Person-ally, I'd like to have a look at that sleazy investigator's apart-ment, and see what's in his car. Eddie said they went over his apartment pretty good but they stuck the car in impound after Eddie rooted around for a few minutes in the garbage that he said was piled up about knee deep."

"Eddie said he'd let you into the impound lot?"

"No, and not the apartment either. We're going to have to do a little B&E."

"Breaking and entering? Are you out of your mind?"

"Don't worry, bro. I'll do the B and we'll both do the E."

"While we're at it, I'd like to have a look at Harvey's computer and also his desk."

"Why is that?" Johnny asked.

"Just a hunch. He's been acting strangely since Haskins was arrested. I've been checking around and Harvey's the one who's been leading the movement to forget Slim Haskins. Instead of being embarrassed for the department because the head football coach was arrested for murder, Harvey seems overjoyed about it."

"OK, the bowl invitations come out Sunday night. Monday you and I will be going crazy trying to keep up, but how about Tuesday night we visit McGrew's apartment?"

Chapter Twenty-Three

Ellen hastily tried pulling open the drawers on Harvey's desk. *Shit*, she thought to herself, every drawer was locked. Jake instructed her to test the drawers and search any that she could get into, and then try getting into any files that she could on Harvey's PC.

Meanwhile, Ellen hoped that Harvey was occupied in Jake's office, the two of them meeting over sandwiches about how they would handle publicity for the upcoming bowl announcement. The lunch meeting was Jake's idea; the plan was to get Harvey out of his office over lunchtime when his assistant was out. Most times when he left the building for lunch, Harvey locked his office but Jake guessed correctly that he wouldn't be as careful if he was just down the hall.

Each second that went by, Ellen felt her muscles grow tighter with tension. She'd only been in Harvey's office for two minutes and already a bead of sweat fell from her forehead onto Harvey's desktop. *Why did she let Jake talk her into doing this?* She was sifting carefully through the papers on top of the desk when a bunch of papers bumped into a cup holding a dozen pens. The cup toppled to the floor and pens scattered around and under the desk.

Ellen stood perfectly still. How loud was that noise? To her it seemed as loud as a jet plane taking off ten feet from Harvey's window. She expected to see everyone on the fourth floor, including Harvey, come running to investigate the crash. She stepped away from the desk and stood motionless for at least thirty seconds. No one came running, so she finished picking up the pens.

Full-blown panic was starting to set in and Ellen's hands were moist. As she jammed the bunch of pens she picked up from the floor into the cup, she saw that her hands were shaking badly.

Screw the desk, it was hopeless. She turned her attention to Harvey's PC monitor. Jackpot! His computer was not only unsecured, but the browser was open to what appeared to be a personal email account. Ellen quickly scanned the inbox...a couple of lovey-dovey notes from Sheila, a few stock tips from what seemed to be an investment broker and that was about it. She opened the sent emails folder and found nothing interesting there either. *This is insane,* she said under her breath.

She had just moved the curser over the deleted emails folder when she heard a booming voice, "What are you doing in my office, Ellen?" Harvey was standing at his office door glaring at her.

"Oh, Mr. Elwood. I was just...uh...there was an email virus going around. James over in IT Services asked me to make sure no one opened it. Since you weren't here, I..."

"Well I'm here now. So I'll take care of it myself."

Starting to regain her composure, Ellen thought quickly and said, "I already deleted it just now. Sorry to go on your computer without you being here but IT said this is a nasty virus and it was urgent to get that email off everyone's system immediately before someone accidentally opened it."

"OK then. I was just coming to get some notes that I forgot. Get back to your desk, or take lunch, or do whatever it is you're supposed to be doing," Harvey said gruffly. He ushered Ellen out of his office. As she was stepping into the hall, she heard Harvey slam his office door and noisily lock it.

***

The day before, Molly had stopped by Jake's office just before five o'clock. She closed the office door and said, "Jake, do you have a minute? There's something on my mind."

"Sure, Molly. We haven't had a chance to talk much lately. The football season has been taking up every waking moment of my time, or so it seems. Is everything going all right on the women's side of things?"

"Oh, yeah, it's been going great. Enthusiasm is still at an all-time high thanks to the football team, in spite of that little problem of the football coach being arrested for murder and led away in shackles. We're having our best year ever so far in women's sports. But that's not why I'm here."

"What is it?"

"The week before the Florida game, I think it was on Monday night, I was working late and had a question I wanted to ask Harvey. I saw his office light was still on and I was just stepping into his outer office, where his assistant sits. I stopped because I heard Harvey and Sheila Elwood arguing in the inner office. They were keeping their voices low but I made out a few words here and there. I swear, it sounded like Sheila was talking about someone being blackmailed. Harvey said something like, 'I'll deal with it.' And then a couple days later that McGrew guy ends up dead. I'm worried."

"Have you told anyone else about this?"

"No, but you know that police detective don't you? Do you think I should talk to him?"

"Not just yet," Jake said, "I'll talk to him first. But give me a day or two. And whatever you do, don't mention this to Harvey."

***

The evening of the day that she was caught snooping in Harvey's office, Jake picked Ellen up for a dinner date. She wasn't even settled in the car seat when Jake said, "What happened when Harvey caught you? What did he say?"

Ellen told Jake every detail and then said, "I don't think he bought my story. He could easily check with IT Services and find out I was lying. I know it was a pretty lame excuse, but it's the best I could come with on the spot. He seemed very irritated, but I would be too if I found someone looking at my computer."

"So the desk was locked? How many locks are on the desk?"

"There's just one lock, right in the middle of the center drawer. It's a wood desk, a nice one. It's kind of sleek and modern."

Jake said, "Hmmm. When I was a kid I used to sneak in my dad's office. He had a wooden desk in his study, one with a lock in the middle like you're describing. If I did something wrong, my dad would sometimes punish me by taking stuff away, candy or little toys. He'd lock them in his desk. I figured out how to pry the desk top up a fraction of an inch, then I'd stick a pen in the gap and turn the lock mechanism to open all the drawers. If Harvey's desk has a design like that, I can get into it. But I'll need to get into his office when there's no one around. And I've got to have some time. It's going to have to be at night."

Ellen was aghast. "Let me get this straight. You're going to break into your boss's office in the dark of night. You and Johnny have both gone off the deep end. You're talking about burglary, even breaking into that dead guy's apartment and his car. You talked me into snooping around Harvey's office and look what happened. This is all based on your hunch that Slim Haskins is innocent, even though everyone in

Springfield and around the whole country thinks he's guilty. Maybe Slim Haskins will be lucky and you'll get picked for jury duty when he goes on trial. You've already decided he's not guilty."

"You're exaggerating, Ellen. I really appreciate you helping me and I'm sorry if you end up getting in trouble over it. But Johnny and I both want to see this through. I won't get you involved anymore."

There were a number of uncomfortable silences during dinner, the first time that ever happened. On their way out of the restaurant, and Jake asked, "Where to?"

"I have an early day tomorrow," Ellen answered, "I think I'm going to turn in and get some sleep."

"Listen," Jake said, "I shouldn't have gotten you tangled up in this. I wish I could explain to you why I'm doing these crazy things but I'm not even sure myself. I guess it boils down to intuition. I looked into Don Haskins' eyes and all I saw was fear and bewilderment. He knows he's being set up, and he has no idea by who or why. I'm also one-hundred percent certain Harvey Elwood is hiding something. At the very least he knows more than he told Eddie. I think he might even be directly involved, I just don't know how."

"I respect your opinion; I really do," Ellen said, "But think about the risks you're taking. If you get caught doing any of these wild stunts that you and Johnny have cooked up, your career could be ruined. You might even go to jail. It just isn't worth the risk, Jake."

Jake smiled at Ellen. "You still don't know me that well yet, baby. When I put my mind to something, I don't fail. Failure is not in the Goodman genes."

Ellen laughed, "OK, Mr. Confidence, I guess I'm not going to change your mind. How about you spend the night at my place? We may as well start practicing for conjugal visits for after you get arrested."

***

After he got home that evening, Harvey told his wife about finding Ellen in his office, then hung his head and waited for the wrath of Sheila to begin. He didn't have to wait long.

"You stupid idiot," Sheila said, "You left your personal email open on your computer and left the room?"

Harvey wondered how a man like him, an ex-NFL player who was six-foot-five and well over two-hundred pounds, could be bullied by a fifty-year-old woman who was a foot shorter and a hundred pounds lighter.

"I was just down the hall in Goodman's office," Harvey pleaded, "and it was lunchtime. No one should have been around."

"Well someone was there. Did you check on the story she gave you?"

Harvey sat mute for a few seconds, building up the courage to answer. This was going to be ugly. "It was a lie. Nobody in IT knew anything about an email virus going around the athletic department."

"You brainless asshole! Tell me now, and tell me the truth: what could she have seen? What was in your email?"

Bad was quickly heading to worse, Harvey thought as he swallowed. "I'm careful about deleting old emails, so the email you sent me where you...you know...talked about taking care of McGrew...that email was deleted. But it was still in my deleted email folder. I realized after, I haven't emptied my deleted email folder in a month or so."

Sheila's head looked like it might explode. Her face was a dark shade of red and her eyes were bulging. Harvey flashed back to his grade school days when he studied mythology. Sheila looked a lot like he imagined Medusa, the evil goddess who could turn a man to stone with her gaze. Sheila let out a loud, long, hissing breath and calmed herself down.

"All right, we need to think this through," Sheila said quietly, "Here's what we know: This girl Ellen had no legitimate reason to be in your office or looking at your PC. Your personal email program was left open. And there was an email in your deleted folder that could send us both to prison. Does that pretty much summarize the situation?"

"I suppose so," Harvey answered.

"Then I don't think we have any choice, darling."

Harvey's heart felt like it stopped beating. "No Sheila, absolutely not. It stops here. I understand you made a terrible mistake with Jennifer, but I forgave you. Then you dragged me into this whole mess with that dirtball private eye. We had to do something about him, you insisted. And I stupidly went along with it. But this girl Ellen, for all we know she didn't see a thing! Plus she's dating Jake Goodman, and he's friends with that police detective. I think Goodman is already suspicious. Killing his girlfriend could open up the whole police investigation again."

"Stop being such a pussy. Do you want to lose everything and go to jail? The sooner we take care of this, the better. I have an idea how to do it..."

***

Jake sat across the desk in Eddie Martin's office and stared at him. Johnny was sitting next to Jake and was glaring at Eddie as well.

Eddie: "You two clowns can give me the stink-eye as long as you want. It's not going to change anything."

Johnny: "Oh really. Have you listened to a word we just said?"

Eddie: "I've listened. Here's what I heard: Molly-someone-or-other, who I don't know from shit, says she overheard bits and pieces of a whispered conversation between two of the most highly respected citizens of our city. And what does she say these pillars of society were discussing? They were conspiring to commit double murder. Did it occur to you that maybe they were talking about what they heard on the news, for Christ's sake? You know, the words *blackmail* and *Ken McGrew* were in the news more than a few times over the past couple of weeks."

Jake: "Molly is as solid as they come. If you knew her you would be taking this more seriously. She doesn't screw around, Eddie. If she says she heard something, then she did."

Johnny: "What's your problem, Eddie?"

Eddie: "The problem is the case is closed! Other than you two shitheads, everyone in town has stopped worrying about who killed those people. Any reasonable person would look at the evidence and know that Slim Haskins did it."

Jake: "What if Haskins is innocent? How can you live with yourself?"

Eddie: "I can't live with losing my job. If I tried to re-open this case without some serious evidence – a lot more than someone overhearing snippets of what could very well be an innocent conversation – I'd be laughed off the detective squad. This isn't my decision, you guys. The Chief told me in no uncertain terms to move on. Haskins will get his day in court, and he'll have a chance to prove he's innocent. I wish him good luck with that."

Johnny: "Then I guess we're on our own."

Eddie: "You guys better not be thinking of doing anything stupid."

Jake: "Do something stupid? Me and Johnny? Of course not, Eddie."

Chapter Twenty-Four

Gazing out his office window at the season's first snow, Harvey Elwood sat at his desk in troubled thought. How did it ever come to this? He remembered back several weeks ago, when he confronted Sheila and she admitted to him that she murdered Jennifer.

Sheila was at Jennifer's apartment building that night intending to force Jennifer to end the affair with Harvey and get an abortion. McGrew found the pregnancy report during his weekly search of Jennifer's apartment and reported his findings to Sheila. An affair was one thing, but now the girl was pregnant and Sheila had to step in and deal with the situation. She suspected Harvey was having an affair with someone and had hired McGrew in late August to find out for certain. By sheer coincidence, Jennifer happened to live in the building that McGrew managed, which resulted in what could well be the easiest private investigation in history. When Sheila learned about Jennifer, she decided to have a revenge affair of her own, and McGrew was a convenient partner.

As she pulled into a parking spot across the street, Sheila was shocked to see Slim Haskins leaving the apartment building. After Haskins drove off, Sheila buzzed McGrew on the intercom and he unlocked the main door for her. She knocked on Jennifer's door but there was no answer, so she tried the knob and found the door was unlocked. She walked in and saw Jennifer laying semi-conscious and moaning on the floor. At that instant, Sheila made the decision to kill the helpless co-ed. A dozen hard blows to her head with a nearby heavy statue were more than sufficient. Since Jennifer was barely conscious, she didn't fight back and only made quiet guttural sounds as Sheila pummeled her.

It was when Sheila did a quick search of the area around Jennifer's body that she found the tiny voice recorder next to her. It must have fallen from pocket of the girl's flannel shirt. She played it and quickly realized Slim Haskins had made himself the perfect patsy by being there earlier. The evidence was on the recorder, anyone who heard it would think he killed the girl. All Sheila needed to do was rewind to the point where she entered the apartment and record silence over that section. With McGrew's help, Sheila cleaned up the apartment to remove traces of her being there and ditched her blood-stained clothes the moment she got home. McGrew carefully edited the security tapes and the police bought his claim that the ancient security system was the reason for the gaps and static in critical parts of the tape.

Harvey remembered his horror and anger when Sheila admitted that she murdered Jennifer. He had great affection for the girl. Sheila sat down with Harvey and calmly explained the situation to him. The girl was pregnant; she was a ticking time bomb that would at some point surely destroy Harvey's career. With Jennifer dead the problem was solved. Sheila also carefully explained her plan to frame Slim Haskins if the police looked like they were getting too close. She told Harvey that he was either all the way in or all the way out. Of course, he could decide to turn her over to the police if that was what he wanted. She painted a vivid and terrible picture to Harvey of that scenario – he would have to admit that his head football coach bludgeoned a co-ed, who was then murdered by the Athletic Director's wife because the girl was pregnant with Harvey's baby. His career would be shattered and he would never work again, there was no doubt. Harvey's decision was a simple one – he would go along with Sheila's plot.

After Jennifer was out of the picture, Sheila rekindled her marriage with Harvey. She despised her husband, but she would keep the dolt happy for the time being and divorce him when the time was right. Sheila lost interest in McGrew, but kept him on the hook, to the point of having sex with him as necessary. The one thing she didn't count on was that the detective would try to blackmail Harvey. At first, McGrew stupidly believed she was going to leave her husband and her lavish lifestyle for a broken-down, middle-aged lush of a private eye. Once McGrew caught on that Sheila was just using him, he decided to make one more score by blackmailing Harvey with the Slim Haskins photos.

Harvey thought the problem of those photos was behind him. When he told Sheila about McGrew's demand for cash, she convinced him that McGrew was a loose end who needed to be eliminated. Ken McGrew knew the secret of how Jennifer really died and it was going to cost a hundred grand to keep him quiet about the photos. Getting rid of him would solve two big problems.

Once the decision was made to kill McGrew, the rest was easy – Sheila dropped by his apartment building and quietly let Harvey into the outer entrance. She fed McGrew a line about wanting to have sex with him, and after he downed a few double Manhattans, they retired to the bedroom. The apartment door was unlocked and McGrew was drunkenly focused on sex, so it was no problem for Harvey to sneak in and smash the detective's head with a baseball bat. That poor slob McGrew never knew what hit him. After they were certain the detective was dead, Sheila checked to make sure the security system was still non-functioning and they took the baseball bat with them. Harvey tossed the baseball bat into the middle of the river on the drive home.

Fortunately the police found the recording of Haskins on McGrew's computer and assumed it was the result of an illegal wiretap of Jennifer's apartment by the sleazy detective. If the police had needed help, Sheila was prepared to send them the pocket recorder anonymously. Harvey had been smart enough to remove the recorder from Slim Haskins' desk before the police were able to get into his office to search it. McGrew had told Sheila all about his blackmail of the football coach and that he had turned the recorder over to him. Sending the recorder to the police turned out to be unnecessary, and the police bit on the idea of Haskins being guilty even faster than Sheila hoped.

Two months seem more like two years; everything happened so quickly, Harvey thought. The timing of all these problems was ironic to say the least. The success of the football team had everyone in the athletic office giddy with excitement for the past two months. Harvey worked to act just as excited as everyone else while at the same time living with the sorrow of Jennifer's death and all the mayhem and scheming that swirled around him.

Harvey hated Sheila more than ever for dragging him into this. For now he'd play along, but as soon as the dust settled he planned to file for divorce.

His thoughts turned to Jake Goodman and this business of his girlfriend snooping around. Sheila was right about not taking any chances with her, as much as Harvey hated to admit it. Obviously, Ellen and Goodman cooked up the scheme to get Harvey out of his office. Even if the girl found something incriminating, all she could do about it was talk to Goodman. Sheila had already arranged to have the disk drive in Harvey's office and home computers removed by a high school computer hacker who lived in their neighborhood. The kid copied only the files Harvey needed and installed new disk drives. He was a good kid that Sheila knew since he was in diapers; he'd keep his mouth shut and happily spend the five hundred dollars he was paid.

***

On Sunday, the bowl invitations were officially announced. Harvey learned the news a few days earlier, because he and Milt were responsible for negotiating the contract for Lincoln State's agreement to play in the bowl. As anticipated, the Abes were playing in Arizona on January third in one of the most important bowl games of the season.

Johnny picked Jake up at ten p.m. and they drove to McGrew's apartment building. As they rode over, Jake asked Johnny, "What do you think of the bowl game?"

"I like the location. I hate winter. It's early December and I'm already freezing my ass off. It'll be colder than shit in Springfield come January and I know I can convince my editor to send me to Phoenix at least five days before the game. So I get to enjoy a week of fun in the sun. But I don't like the match-up in the game at all. We're playing Utah. They have a great record, one loss just like us, but I'd much rather that we were playing a big-name school."

"It seems to happen a lot that the non-BCS schools end up playing one another in big bowl games," Jake said, "Remember, we're an outsider and so is Utah. They make us play each other instead of a big-name school. That way whoever wins, the big schools will claim it was a lightweight matchup and either Lincoln State or Utah would have gotten trampled against a major conference school."

"Yeah, they don't want a repeat of Boise State against Oklahoma or Wisconsin against Texas Christian. Those were major bowl upsets by non-BCS schools against the big boys. If there were more of those upsets, people would be screaming to change the bowl selection rules to be fairer to small schools."

"So they put Lincoln State and Utah in a situation where, no matter which team ends up winning, they won't be taken seriously."

"You know what else is irritating?" Johnny said, "I remember when bowl games used to come to a climax on New Year's Day. It was so great, a fourteen-hour day of college football gluttony. I used to love that. Now the TV networks make the bowls space their schedules out so there's only one – maybe two – bowls on TV at any moment."

Jake laughed, "I think you're picking shit with the chickens on that complaint, buddy. Personally, I like it that way. I get to see all the major bowl games spread out over a week or so and that way I can watch them all."

Johnny parked across the street from McGrew's building entrance and they waited for twenty minutes until someone approached the main building entrance.

"There! That guy is heading for the door!" Johnny said, and jogged casually across the street. "Hey neighbor, how you doin'?"

The building resident glanced at Johnny and nodded while

he unlocked the door. Johnny grabbed the door while it was open and walked in behind the man. After the resident turned the corner and started down the hall, Johnny held the door open and waved to Jake.

"Piece of cake, man. We're in." Johnny said.

"No we're not," Jake answered, "we still have to get into the apartment."

Johnny pulled a set of pick-locks from his pocket. "We'll be in before you know it. You just keep a lookout for anyone coming down the hall. Which apartment is McGrew's?"

"How should I know? I was never there. Jesus, Johnny."

"OK, go to the mailboxes and look for McGrew's name on a mailbox. He was the manager, so maybe it'll say that somewhere."

Jake went to the mailboxes and found nothing indicating which apartment was McGrew's or the building manager's. All he could find were three mailboxes that looked like the name was recently removed. He trotted back down the hall and said, "It's gotta be one of these three."

"I vote for apartment number 101. That number sounds like the manager would live there, doesn't it?" Johnny went to the door with picks in hand. He held them up to the light to select one that looked close in size to the lock and pushed it into the deadbolt.

"Wait!" Jake whispered, "I think I hear a TV going in there!"

At that instant a very large and burly male student cracked open the door. Johnny quickly withdrew the pick from the lock.

"What the fuck are you doing?" the student asked.

"Sorry man, my friend and I went out for a few beers and I lost my goddamned apartment key. I just moved in last week, I got confused which apartment was mine. Which is the resident manager's apartment? Maybe he can let me in."

"It's 108, but the manager's dead and the apartment's vacant. They still haven't cleaned out the mess or hired a new manager. You missed the excitement; there have been two murders in this building so far this school year. There's a phone number posted by the mailboxes for emergencies. I think the landlord lives in Peoria so you'll have to wait a while if you need help. I've got an exam tomorrow or I'd let you hang out here."

"We'll just go to my buddy's place until I find my key," Johnny said, "Thanks for your help, man, sorry to bother you."

The pair headed for number 108 and Johnny pulled his picks out again. "Now let me show you how it's done."

Fifteen minutes later, with Johnny's forehead dripping sweat and the door still locked, Jake couldn't resist saying, "Is this really how it's done?"

"Shut up. I almost got it. There!" Johnny swung the door open. "Holy shit, it stinks in here!" Johnny said, "McGrew was a pig."

"The place is almost empty," Jake said, "there's not much left."

They walked around the apartment. "You take the bedroom and I'll take the living room. When we're done we'll both look through the third room. It looks like an office, only dirtier."

Jake searched the small bedroom. The mattress was gone but blood was splattered in a five-foot semi-circle on the wall at the head of the bed. The bloodstain looked like a macabre headboard. The threadbare carpet was full of blood stains all around the bed. Jake opened drawers in the dresser and nightstand and searched carefully. There was absolutely nothing but a few pieces of clothing.

"The police have really cleaned this place out," Jake called to Johnny.

"I'm not finding anything either, just dust and dirt. Let's try the office."

There was a file cabinet that was empty except for a few manila folders with nothing in them. Jake turned his attention to the desk and opened the drawers one by one. Most were empty, but the shallow, wide middle drawer had a layer of paperclips, pencils, pens and other office items. Jake ran his hands around the bottom of the drawer. "Ouch! He had a lot of thumb tacks," Jake said, "Hey! What's this?" Back in the far back corner, his fingernail scraped the edge of something that felt like a business card. Jake worked his fingernail under it and pulled the card up and out of the drawer.

"Here's a phone number," Jake said, "It looks like it's written on a piece of an index card, a local area code, looks like a cell number."

"Keep it, we'll do a reverse search on the number later," Johnny said, "It's probably nothing but you never know."

After another ten minutes of searching, Jake said, "We're pushing our luck being here and I really don't think there's anything."

"You're right. Good job, partner. It's Miller Time." Jake put the paper with the phone number in his wallet.

As their first beer arrived, Johnny said, "That was disappointing. The cops really cleaned the place out. I'm surprised Eddie didn't come up with anything. Unless...and I hate to say this...unless he's right and Slim Haskins is the killer."

Jake frowned, "I know, this is frustrating. But I'd still like to have a look at Harvey's desk before I give up. Are you going to look at McGrew's car?"

"Hell, yes!" Johnny said, "This is fun, man! Besides, I still think Haskins is innocent."

***

Harvey suggested a late afternoon meeting with Jake to outline the initial plans for the bowl game. After the plans were laid out, Harvey changed the subject.

"Jake, I'm sure your friend Ellen told you about me catching her in my office. Someone violating my private office is very serious. I've also heard rumors that you think Slim Haskins has been wrongfully accused."

Fortunately, Jake had anticipated this discussion. He knew Harvey would be suspicious about Jake's involvement with Ellen snooping in his office. "I believe anyone, including Don Haskins, is innocent until proven guilty. My only concern is that everyone around the athletic office has already tried and convicted him. I think that's wrong, and that's what I've told people. As far as Ellen, I can't even guess why she was in your office. She told me it had something to do with a computer virus."

"Hummph. You're a sharp young man, Jake, and you could have a great career ahead of you, but you have some things to learn. I'm planning to retire in four or five years. Molly desperately wants the A.D. job but she's a woman, and a dyke to boot – she doesn't have a prayer of becoming Athletic Director. Milt wants the job too, but he's a dipshit, he would run the department into the crapper and the board knows it. Frankly, I think you'd be great in this job. You'll still be a little young, even in five years, but I'm sure I can convince the board to promote you. They'll listen to me. But you need to learn who your friends are – who can help you in your career. That's the smart thing to do. Are we on the same page?"

Jake went along with the charade and said mechanically, "We are on the same page, Harvey. I appreciate your confidence in me, and I respect your advice."

"Good, good," Harvey said absent-mindedly, "Keep up the good work."

Jake left Harvey's office convinced more than ever that Harvey was deeply involved in the murders.

Sitting at his desk watching Jake leave, Harvey was certain that Ellen needed to be silenced. He picked up his phone and dialed Sheila's cell number.

Chapter Twenty-Five

Jake hadn't heard from Johnny Rose in nearly a week, which suited him fine. Basketball season was heading into full swing and he was fully occupied keeping up with that. He worked late every evening in the hope that Harvey would leave his office unattended and make it easy to search his desk. For the past week, Harvey worked so late that he outlasted everyone else in the office, including Jake.

Johnny called Thursday afternoon with good news. "I finally got a line on where McGrew's car is located in the impound lot. The cops are done with it and the city is holding it until a relative claims it, like someone wants that piece of crap. I used to drive that same model back in high school, and it was a used one back then – that's how old that car is."

"So when are you going to look at it?

"Tonight about six o'clock, as soon as the night shift guy takes over. I have a line of bullshit ready to give the security guard at the impound entrance. I may need to slip him a few bucks, but I'll get in. How about you? Any luck with Harvey's office?"

"Harvey's been working late every night."

"Want to come along with me?"

"No, I'm going to stay late again this evening and try one more time."

"All right, talk to you after I check out McGrew's car."

Jake pushed the end-call button and saw the low-battery indicator on his phone glowing. *Damn, I forgot to charge it last night.* There were three inches of freshly fallen snow on the ground and the last thing Jake felt like doing was walking from his warm office out to the parking lot. But the only charger he had with him was plugged into his car power. He trudged through the snow and connected his phone to the charger. He hated winter. It was only four-thirty and already almost dark, he thought disgustedly. He hurried back to his office to get out of the snow and cold, cursing his forgetfulness and Midwest winters the whole time.

At six, Jake got up from his desk and casually walked by Harvey's office. The outer door was closed, but a quick glance showed the door to Harvey's inner office was open and dark. It looked like this was his chance. Jake slid his key into the outer office door and tried to turn it. It didn't work! He thought all the outer office keys were supposed to be the same, or so he had been told.

At that moment the night custodian appeared around the corner. Jake knew him by name because they frequently bumped into one another at odd hours. "Hey, Jerry," Jake said, "Harvey's assistant left a report she was supposed to give me on her desk. I really need it tonight. Can you let me in?"

"Sure, Mr. Goodman," Jerry said, and opened the door. "Just close 'er up when you're done, and I'll swing by in a while to lock it," he said over his shoulder as he walked away.

***

Johnny walked through the impound lot toward Ken McGrew's car. All it took to get in was his business card and a couple of twenties to the security guard.

McGrew's Oldsmobile sedan had an interior that could easily fit a family of five and still have room for a couple of Golden Retrievers. The doors were all unlocked and the trunk was closed but unlocked. Johnny brushed off the snow, lifted the trunk lid, and turned his head at the stench. Jesus, did this guy not know what a garbage can was? It looked like months of fast food containers. Johnny held his breath and started sorting through the debris. He pushed the fast food wrappers to one side and saw a dozen manila files strewn beneath the clutter.

***

Jake eased into Harvey's office and turned on the desk lamp instead of the overhead light. The next step was to crack open the desk. Sure enough, it was the same design as his father's old desk and he had it open in just over a minute. He started with the drawer on the lower left and methodically worked his way through each one. He found absolutely nothing of interest until the top right drawer.

Jake opened the drawer and felt the contents inside. Immediately he noticed the bottom surface of the drawer felt different from its counterpart on the left side of the desk. He opened both drawers and simultaneously felt the bottoms with each hand. The right drawer definitely was different; the bottom was rougher and seemed a bit higher than the left-hand drawer. Jake picked up the desk lamp and shone it into the wide-open drawer. To Jake's surprise, he found it was a "secret drawer."

When Jake was a teen, he and his friends used what they called a "secret drawer" to hide things from their parents. It was a simple, yet elegant, design. Cut a thin board just slightly narrower than the exact width of the drawer, and about a half-inch shorter. Then cut two square rods or dowels about three-quarters or one inch in diameter (depending on how much hiding space was needed) to the length of the drawer, and glue each to the bottom of the drawer, tight against each side. Now simply rest the cut board on top of the rods and you have a convenient hiding spot in the bottom of the drawer. Growing up, Jake found it the perfect size for *Playboy* magazines in his middle school days, and kept joints in there during his high school drug-experimentation period. If done carefully with the right materials, the compartment was almost undetectable, especially if the visible part of the drawer had lots of stuff in it. Unless someone was looking for it and carefully compared it to other drawers, like Jake did, they would never find it.

***

Johnny picked up the first folder and opened it. Between the small light in McGrew's trunk and a flashlight he brought with him, he could read the files in the dark. The first folder he picked up had stuff in it that was over a year old. What a filing system, Johnny thought. He picked up another folder. It was similar; all the papers were dated from over a year earlier. As disorganized as the filing system was, each folder was neatly kept and included a daily log of what work McGrew did on a case, how many hours were spent, and what his findings were. Johnny scanned through each folder and found nothing interesting.

The front seat area was clean and the glove compartment was empty. He moved to the back seat, which was as full of garbage and disgusting as the trunk.

***

Jake quickly emptied the drawer contents and pulled up the false bottom. Underneath were two identical voice recorders and a bank funds transfer form. Jake pressed rewind on the first recorder and played it. Nothing. He did the same with the second and heard Slim Haskins and Jennifer arguing – the same recording he heard in Eddie's office. Why would Harvey have that recorder since McGrew was the one blackmailing Slim Haskins? Jake picked up the bank form and held it to the light. It was for a hundred thousand dollars, made out to Theodore McGrew with some account numbers filled in beneath. It was dated several weeks earlier but never signed by Harvey, so obviously the transfer was never made.

Suddenly Jake remembered the scrap of paper he found in McGrew's apartment. He used Harvey's desk phone to dial the number. It rang once then went to voicemail, saying "This is Sheila Elwood. I can't answer right now...."

It took a minute to digest the information, but then Jake hurriedly cleaned up Harvey's office and bounded down the stairs to the parking lot. He needed to call Johnny. He picked up his phone and saw two messages from Ellen, one at six-fifteen and the other at seven o'clock, just a minute before. He dialed voicemail.

***

In McGrew's back seat Johnny sorted carefully through greasy fast food containers, old newspapers, petrified peach pits and very smelly apple cores. He found nothing. Then an idea hit him. When he drove the same car back in high school, Johnny took advantage of a hiding place specific to this model. Half of the back seat folded down on itself to allow long objects to be carried in the trunk. On the side of the back cushion was a zipper that allowed access to the foam padding inside. Why it was there, Johnny had no idea, but he found it came in handy for stashing condoms.

Johnny opened the zipper and was surprised to find another manila folder wedged between the foam padding and the vinyl seat covering. He pulled it out and shined his flashlight on it. The tab said *Sheila Elwood*. How did McGrew know her? Johnny thought. Like all his files, McGrew kept a log. Apparently the detective had been hired by Sheila to trail Harvey. The log detailed Harvey's visits to Jennifer's apartment, dates and times he came and went. As Johnny read on, the notes became more personal and it turned into more of a diary describing McGrew's affair with Sheila.

Scrawled at the bottom of the last page of the log was:

If something happens to me I hope this is found. Sheila Elwood killed Jennifer Stewart. I'm getting out of town as soon as I can. Sheila is acting crazier by the day. The shit will hit the fan sometime soon.

***

The first call on Jake's voicemail said, "Hi Jake, it's Ellen. Harvey Elwood called me a few minutes ago. He wants to meet at seven tonight regarding a big job promotion. It's has to do with women's soccer – you know that's why I've been working at my stupid office job in the department, hoping an opportunity would open up in soccer. I was worried at first, but Harvey said Molly would be there too so I think it's OK. We're meeting at that small soccer building over by the practice field. You know, the place where they store all the balls and equipment? I'll call you after. Bye."

The second call said, "Me again, Jake. Where are you? Anyway, I'm just stepping into my meeting. Wish me luck!"

***

He was still holding the file when the sound of his cell phone ringing made Johnny jump. "It's Jake! Drop everything and get to that small building by the soccer practice fields. Take a right on the first street past the main soccer stadium and look for my car. I think Ellen's in trouble. Hurry!"

With the file folder in hand Johnny sprinted through the impound lot and out the entrance. He started his car and fishtailed through the snowy parking lot into the street and toward the soccer complex.

When Johnny arrived, Jake was parked on road that passed the soccer practice fields. He waved at Johnny to stop and shouted, "There's no road to get our cars near the building, we'll have to run across the field." Johnny leaped out of his car and they ran toward the small building.

Harvey had driven his SUV across the snowy field and was parked near the side of the building. Jake saw a light on and crept slowly up to the one window to peek inside. His heart skipped a beat at what he saw. Molly wasn't there. Instead he saw Harvey, Ellen and Sheila Elwood. He whispered to Johnny, "Sheila and Harvey have Ellen cornered in there. They're standing between Ellen and the door. The room is about twenty-by-fifteen feet, a pile of soccer balls in one corner and a couple of small tables in the other corner. Harvey's holding a large knife, but it doesn't look like Sheila has a weapon. Harvey's about seven feet inside the door straight ahead, Sheila about five feet to this left."

"Let's bust in," Johnny said, "We'll both go for Harvey and after he's under control we'll get Sheila."

"You go low at his knees and I'll go for the knife. On the count of three, buddy. Here we go!"

The door burst open and Johnny landed a hard shoulder into Harvey's knees. Harvey yelled in pain as he went down. In the meantime, Jake pushed Harvey's hand that held the knife with a violent motion. As Harvey's hand hit the concrete floor, the knife came loose and skidded into a corner.

Jake turned his attention to Sheila. "She has a gun!" Jake shouted as Sheila pulled a thirty-eight from her waistband. Sheila raised the gun and was in position to fire at Johnny when a soccer ball rocketed across the room. The ball hit Sheila squarely in the middle of her face. She dropped the gun and fell dazed to her knees, blood pouring from her nose. Within a few seconds of her initial kick, Ellen followed up with a hard right foot directly into Sheila's sternum. She collapsed in a moaning heap on the floor.

Johnny outweighed Harvey by eighty pounds and used his heft to keep Harvey pinned to the floor. Ellen picked up the gun and pointed it loosely toward both Harvey and Sheila. Jake pulled out his phone and dialed Eddie's number.

"Eddie, it's Jake Goodman. Get over to the soccer practice fields right away, and bring a squad car with you. Harvey and Sheila Elwood just tried to kill Ellen and we have evidence they murdered Ken McGrew and Jennifer Stewart."

"Are you serious?"

"Get over here fast. Look for the lights on in a small building in the middle of the practice complex."

Chapter Twenty-Six

"Here's to not giving up on what you believe," Eddie said as he raised his glass to the other five people at the table.

"And here's to believing your friends if the same situation should happen again," Johnny answered with a smile. Johnny's date elbowed him hard in the ribs.

"It's alright to remind me," Eddie answered, "I'm hardly ever wrong so I don't mind admitting it when I am. That's what tonight's all about. "

Eddie had invited Jake, Ellen, and Johnny to dinner at Maldaner's Restaurant to celebrate solving the case but also to make up for his misjudgment about Slim Haskins' innocence. With the hectic schedule surrounding the Abes' bowl appearance, Jake suggested they wait until after the holidays and the game were finished.

"Sheila and Harvey have been in jail for about a month now. What's happening with their case?" Jake asked.

"We've developed a ton of evidence against them. It turned out Sheila's DNA was all over Jennifer Stewart's clothing. And of course Harvey and Sheila's DNA was in McGrew's bedroom. We just didn't have anything to match it to until they were arrested. Of course we have your three statements and the evidence you dug up."

"I read that they both confessed," Ellen said.

"More like rolled over on one another," Eddie answered, "They weren't in custody more than an hour when they offered to testify against each other for a better deal."

"I feel so stupid falling for that phony excuse they used on me," Ellen said.

"No, you weren't stupid at all," Jake said, "Sheila was a master manipulator. Harvey knew you wanted a job in the soccer program more than anything. She got him to use that against you."

"I know this sounds ridiculous," Ellen said, "But I feel a little sorry for Harvey. Yes, he had an affair with a student, which is terrible. But he really did care for Jennifer. He got pulled into this mess by Sheila."

"He could've said no to Sheila. If you saw McGrew's body you wouldn't feel bad for Harvey. That was a brutal killing," Eddie said.

"How much time will they get, Eddie?" Johnny said.

"The D.A. is going for second degree against Sheila on Jennifer and first degree for both her and Harvey on McGrew. Harvey's also an accessory after the fact on the first murder. Then the D.A. tacked on conspiracy and some other charges just for fun. I'd say twenty years minimum, probably more. " Eddie turned to Jake and Ellen, "How are things at the athletic department?"

"The teams are doing great. As you know, we beat Utah in the bowl game, and both the men's and women's basketball teams are doing fantastic so far. But the administration is in a complete shambles. Molly has been appointed Interim Athletic Director, but the board has formed a search committee to look for a permanent replacement so it's unlikely she'll keep the job," Jake said.

"Out of the Football Bowl Subdivision college programs, there's only a handful of women Athletic Directors," Ellen added, "So she has an uphill battle if she wants to be a head Athletic Director."

"You're right, and Molly is very upset about it. She's made no effort to hide that she's applying to every school that has an opening," Jake said, "I don't think Milt stands a chance of getting it either. The board wants to clean house and get a fresh start. Even with the success we've had on the field, this scandal has badly damaged the school's reputation. I'm not confident that I'll be around long unless Molly ends up getting the Athletic Director position."

"That was a nice thing you did for Slim Haskins at the bowl game," Ellen said to Johnny, "getting him a field press pass so he could at least stand on the sideline."

"It seemed like the right thing to do," Johnny said, "the university really hung him out to dry. Even after the murder charges were dropped, all the blackmail stuff was made public and that killed his chances. The university not only refused to reinstate him as coach, they wouldn't even help him get to the bowl game. So I did what I could. When they found out I got him the pass, the school actually got a court order barring him from talking to any player or coach; but at least he was there. I didn't make any friends doing that."

"Haskins got his hundred grand back from McGrew's estate," Eddie said, "and with the success Lincoln State had this season he'll probably land somewhere, even with all his baggage. Not at a major program, probably a smaller school. He'll come out OK."

"Speaking of job security," Johnny said, "I get this vibe that I'm about as popular as a nun at a bachelor party at the newspaper these days. The Editor in Chief told me I was supposed to stay out of the case and he is very disappointed that I didn't follow orders. And getting Haskins that on-field pass for the bowl game really rubbed some people the wrong way."

"That doesn't seem right; you're a hero, baby!" Johnny's date said, throwing her arms around him dramatically.

"Being a hero isn't always as impressive as you think it's going to be," Johnny said with a smile at Jake.

"I got an interesting call this week," Jake said, "It was from the top guy in the United States for FIVA, you know the European soccer organization that holds the big World Trophy soccer tournament? Their next worldwide tournament is in a couple of years and it's going to be held in New York. They want to interview me to be in charge managing their entire Public Relations operation in the U.S."

"That's great news, Jake!" Ellen said, but a quick look showed she wasn't thrilled with the prospect of Jake leaving Illinois.

"If I get hired, I'll have complete authority in building a staff," Jake said as he looked at Ellen, "I'm sure that there will be a well-paid opening you're qualified for." Then he turned to Johnny, "and I bet we'll need a world-class sports writer on staff too."

"I don't suppose they'll need someone to manage security?" Eddie asked.

"You never know, Eddie, you never know," Jake answered, as he raised his glass to the table.